Still, Life:
a collection of echoes

by
Melissa Volker

1st edition 2016

Little Dory Press
ISBN: 978-0692679661

To New York City: you insane, beautiful, infuriating, magical, horrendous place. You planted seeds. You fed my soul at the same time that you drained it. I loved you and I hated you, and were it *not* for you, none of these stories would have gotten told.

Acknowledgments

Thank you ad-infinitum to Robin Meloy Goldsby (robin.goldsby.de) for her remarkable patience with my constant requests for advice and input, for her time, attention and support, and for being an amazing, creative woman and the best cross-continental, multi-decade friend. You are the best!

Thanks to Robin Spielberg (www.robinspielberg.com) for her time, input, tolerance of my never-ending questions, boundless enthusiasm and support. I am constantly inspired!

Most importantly -- to my family: my husband, Chris, for his patience and support through the entire process of writing, rewriting, and everything that comes afterward -- I love you. My mom, for encouragement. And to my son, Lex -- thank you for thinking it's cool that I'm a writer, for coming to my events, and basically just being as awesome as you are -- you inspire me to be better.

Dad: wish you were here.

AUTHOR INTRODUCTION

All these stories were written during my time living, working, struggling, loving and hating the elusive and enigmatic city of New York in the 1980s.

At that time, the Twin Towers were still there -- those truly iconic, dizzying, shining, impossibly tall monoliths rising up from the grime and pain as though pointing the way for everyone who ventured into that city's embrace.

Up.

Look up. When you don't get the part, the gig, the job; when you lose your apartment, your lover, your hope...

Look up.

They were there, at first just two more skyscrapers pushing their way free, breaking the invisible ceiling of dirt and smog and noise, but they quickly became a symbol of that city itself.

The Towers and the City were one and the same.

Stand at their base, chin to the glass and look up -- it made you dizzy

While I did not live there when they came down, it didn't matter -- once you've lived there (and for as long as I did) -- it is forever a part of you. Like the dirt and steam get in your pores, the stink of subway in your clothes, once there, New York City is forever part of your very being.

So when they came down, I felt it. Right to my core.

And so, finally, love it, hate it -- and I did both, these stories are a love letter to a city that molded me, forged me, inspired and destroyed me, and that in the end, felt its own pain at having a piece of its spirit torn away.

And yet, like so many of us that were once a part of her, came back stronger.

BOOK ONE

GATSBY REVISITED

I have always wanted to live The Great Gatsby in that carnival, dervish, seductive world of Fitzgerald. But I am born easily seventy years too late, I am not rich -- nor do I know anyone who is -- and although I did have the decadence once, I do not recall it as being quite the same.

I have always wanted to be the part of Daisy that is forever cool and powdered when all about her is wilting. The part that appears angelic and laughing and shaded with soft pink light when all about her falls heavy and dark and eternally earth-bound.

There is no way to be shocking anymore. Not really. No equivalent to the rebellion of dancing the Charleston with your skirt flapping and spinning to allow a glimpse of rolled stocking. Pierced tongues are somehow lacking the devilish innocence of rolled stockings and too many martinis. Do I romanticize it all, do you think? Perhaps. But that was always the point, wasn't it?

And that, too, is sorely lacking. We've grown too wise, to

cynical, too bored.

Yes, I would like to live the life of the Great American Novel, but the world doesn't seem to have room for that anymore.

Where does this fascination, preoccupation, obsession, compulsion, and love affair with Gatsby come from, you ask? Probably from the constant reminder of my last name -- Buchannan. And although I am quite certain my English-teacher parents contemplated completing the tragic fantasy in my first name, they settled instead on a character from my mother's favorite movie: Holly. Holly Buchannan. That's me. And in truth, the influence of my first name is apparent as well. Whereas I long for Daisy's ethereal countenance, I also yearn for Holly's devil-may-care soul. Even though both were masks and illusion. The world is full of illusion, isn't it?

In my mind, I am surrounded by the light reflected off a dozen bouquets of white roses, my name uttered softly by carefully spoken voices, the rain falling through summer leaves disguising my sad, loving, lost tears.

In reality, I am the woman beside you, digging for her keys as she waits for the light to cross the street on her way to work at the bookstore.

When I have the little girl I know I will never have I am going to name her something that's never been written anywhere, or spoken over a glass of champagne, or shouted into the wind and rain and moors by a fictional character. Of course, first I will have to meet and marry the father of such a child. Although, that's not quite right, is it? I mean, you don't have to marry a man to have his child now, do you?

I smoke a cigar. I should mention that now. Not a big, fat,

smelly stogie of stout old-timers hunched over a single malt scotch no ice, in dark, wood-paneled bars. But a small, slender one, just enough to be incongruent. Just enough to elicit a stare or two. When I am older I want to smoke a corn cob pipe. I can't do it now. It would just be silly. When you are old, you are eccentric, when you are young, you are just a freak. I read that somewhere. Or, maybe I wrote it. Either one is possible.

When I am not smoking a cigar, I return to cigarettes, carried in a small, antique case, a la old black and white movies. They are difficult to find now, those cases -- unless you go-lightly to Tiffany's and spend a thousand dollars. Please!

Do you remember the scene in the movie The Great Gatsby when Robert Redford's Gatsby put on his old uniform, lit one candle in the center of the floor, and danced Mia Farrow's Daisy around the room in silent, poignant memory? I do. I do.

I am telling you an awful lot about myself and my secrets, but it is true what they say -- it is easier to talk to a stranger. Especially a faceless one. But even though you are faceless, I know you are kind. I can tell those things, you know. Don't ask me how. I just can. And isn't easier hearing personal things from someone just as faceless? The barrier of the printed page is a transcendent one. There is courage in anonymity.

Before I go any further, I should assure you that I am well aware that Daisy is a tragic figure in literature. They all were. Are. But that doesn't make them any less appealing.

Well, now you know something about me. Quite a lot, actually. At least what's truly important to know. But please, do not feel the need to return the favor. Indeed, I prefer you to remain a stranger to me. Just a silent listener out there in the darkness of the world beyond the boundaries of the page. If you become too familiar, I won't want to share anymore. And I do. Want to share more.

It is hot. It is August in New York and that always means it is hot. The air is heavy and steaming and makes my dress cling to me with a collection of a million tiny beads of sweat. As many beads of sweat as there are stars in the sky. Stars that you almost never see in the city, isn't that right? Although, I did see them one miraculous night in winter. Up on the roof of the little shoebox building I live in. The sky was cobalt, the moon in the middle of a total eclipse, and I stood in the doorway, half in, half out in the cold, crisp air. I saw Orion, clear as if I had hung him there myself. I was like a child, amazed and awed. It looked like it was etched on glass.

I try to recall the clear coolness of the sky, the bite of the late night winter breeze. But the heat is too oppressive.

These are days to be spent in museums, marble floored with high, cool stone walls, and the pervasive, perfect silence. I prefer the Metropolitan Museum of Art because there one can transcend time. The massive, stone stairway inside seems the one Cinderella lost her slipper on, and once at its top, all around you are collections of centuries. It is a great, columned time machine, each doorway a portal to another place in history. I stroll through ancient Egypt, the great stone sphinx eyeing me with their all-knowing, secret-keeping gazes. I fall into the pastel, cataract blossoms of Monet and see myself reclined in a row boat gently wafting downstream in the soft air of spring. I sit on a bench in a Chinese garden, sculpted and sparse and serene. And at the Rembrandts, I flirt with pale-faced gentlemen with the sound of harpsichord music drifting through the rooms.

Impossible tapestries, armor for men and beast, ornately carved ivory and wood pistols far too pretty to ever fire upon anyone, or to have the power to take a life, and spindly rapiers with jewel-encrusted hilts. Bustiers, corsets, hoops and velvet, all manner of dress and style!

And even full of people wandering lost and dreamy, it remains unexpectedly quiet. Almost as soothing as the sacred silence of the church. I have often considered losing myself in there, among the Greek statues or Egyptian mummies, leaving me to wander forever through the endless halls of memory and time. But then what of the rest of the world? The world beyond the columns and scrolls and amulets. I'd like to think it would not be the same were I to lose myself in the labyrinth of time. Would it? Be the same, do you think, were I not a part of it? However small? Well, perhaps it would. And so perhaps the next time I visit the great stone time machine on Eighty-First and Fifth I will, indeed, climb into a sarcophagus and view the world from a tomb for a while.

I have tried the Museum of Modern Art, but I find I spend a great deal of time before massive canvases painted all white save for one six inch strip a third of the way across running vertically down, with my brow knitted and my lips pursed and a totally unselfconscious look of bewilderment on my face.

The same for the one that is truly immense, floor to ceiling, all crimson red except for one black coat button directly in the center. I try, truly I do, to let it move me, direct me, fill me.

But I cannot escape the thought that if I dunked my soup ladle in chartreuse paint and hung it on a shocking pink backboard I, too, could hang in MOMA. Perhaps I am uncultured. Uneducated. Limited. Perhaps I am the only one who really knows what's going on. Perhaps it doesn't matter. I mean, Campbell's soups cans -- who would have thought? But there it is. He just thought of it first. What color is chartreuse, exactly? And puce, too, while we're on the subject.

And when did clothing companies decide to start giving colors the name of food? Celery, Tangerine, Wheat...I'm sorry, I digress...

Out in front of the Met I sit on the edge of the water fountain, ignoring the occasional spray across my face while trying to eat a Dove bar before the sun gets it. It is, in truth, a hopeless battle, and the most I can do is try to avoid heavy, melted corners of chocolate as they slide away from the ice cream toward my skirt. Actually, I'd like a smoke, but it is so unbearably hot, the thought of lighting something on fire and keeping it nearby is a ridiculous consideration. So, it is me and my ice cream as I move to a bench slightly protected by shade near an elderly woman selling her own paintings. I can't tell what they are, sort of city silhouettes at sunset that look as if they've been left in the sun, the colors of sunset and shadow smearing into one another. They're not really very good, but one of them, all red and orange and brown smudges makes me somehow sad in a full, quiet way and so I give her five dollars for it. I think, as I hold it in my lap, it would be perfectly at home next to the immense crimson canvas with the single black button. Moreso, even.

I realize that perhaps I should have bought one with more

blues and greys to inspire a little cool thinking, but those felt empty and desolate, and I like the sadness this one radiates.

On the way back home, I pass a homeless man who has set up a makeshift, but heartfelt home in a service entrance. He sits on a chair against the wall of the building, left leg crossed casually over the other, elbow propped on a cardboard box table looking as though he was expecting very special company. I take my wonderfully sad picture and place it on the cardboard box table so it, too, leans against the building. He looks at it, at me, claps his hands together in genuine delight and says, "That is exactly what that space needed!", and returns to his waiting as if nothing out of the ordinary had occurred. Sort of the way Daisy looked when she turned to face Gatsby in Nick's house for the first time in so many years.

An angel reached down and placed a touch of sweetness in his world, and it was as though he had been expecting it all along. Perhaps he had.

I laughed with him, and for a long time after I left him, my heart full of bubbles that had no other way out. His delight made me dizzy. As the heat makes me dizzy, and often times I catch a sense of the world spinning, and that, my dear, strange friend, is the best dizziness of all.

Do you think it strange that I wasn't saddened by this poor, shabby man and his cardboard box? Well, I have two things to say about that. His delight in my gift made me sad in the same way the painting itself did. Warm and full and honest. Yet, although I find it horrendous that any soul should have to live without the basic allowances of life, he did not seem unhappy in his existence. Perhaps he chose it.

Perhaps he thinks he is currently sitting in Versailles awaiting the arrival of his exquisite princess and bride to be? Whatever the truth, it is also true that he was sincerely happy. How many of us can say that? And so I can be nothing but happy for him. How dare I do any less? To feel anything short of that would be to pass judgment. And that is not my place. Nor yours.

I sit by the river, staring at the cobble-like stone beneath my feet. Where are the dreamers and lovers of life and language? Have we, indeed, come so far that they are things too basic for our sophisticated, educated, evolved souls? Or is it that the world has gone the other way; we are moving too fast, have stopped paying attention, gotten too selfish?

What would Fitzgerald write about me, I wonder? Would he paint a picture as pastel and delicate and fragile and bored and lost and beautiful and tragic and childish as his beloved Daisy? And would he write for me a love as powerful, hopeless, unendurable, and impossible as Gatsby's?

Perhaps he has. Or someone like him. Perhaps I am, darling stranger, no more than a character of some dreamers dream. A lover of life and language, of the magic of painting with words. Perhaps all of us, in our hopeless, hapless, illusions of life are no more than that.

Let me ask you, now that I feel so completely at ease with you, my friend out there in the dark beyond the page, would she ever smoke a cigar, do you think? If she were today as I am?

Someday, I do believe I shall have to ask her.

IT'S A WONDERFUL TOWN

New York is a cavalcade of experiences; a carnival of emotions and sensations ranging from the electric, eclectic insanity of neon and nightlife and danger, to the sad, deprived isolation of desolate, rain-swept streets lit by circle after lonely circle of streetlights, with lost dreams and empty bottles strewn in the gutters -- waiting, waiting, to be washed away.

I have personally seen, passed through, and lived both sides of the tarnished coin. In fact, my life appears to pass through each with some regularity, like the gentle, constant sway of a pendulum.

I am at once the frail, sensitive, passionate artist -- touched by all, pained by all -- and the fighting, cold, oblivious Manhattan-ite here only to take and enjoy what is rightfully mine; either one subject to appear at a moment's notice.

Either pair of eyes subject to seeing without prior warning.

Like one of those dolls whose head spins to reveal two different faces.

Thinking on that, I realize that I seem to have little control over just what pair of eyes, or rather, what lens I view through at any given moment. The mood I wake with often dictates. Or the quality of light seeping under my blinds when I first open my eyes. Perhaps even dreams play a hand in what manner I will view the world when I first set my eyes upon it each day: glittering, wild promise, or stifling hollow disappointment.

The winter months I am something of a bear. Not in spirit, but in behavior. I am prone to longer sleep and less activity and am much happier in the warmth of my heated abode than in the frigid, wind-whipped streets.

In this cement garden, the pure whiteness of the first snowfall lasts no more than an hour at most, and if it isn't caught before the first signs of morning traffic, it is lost forever in grey slush and gutter puddles.

I have been fortunate enough to witness one or two of those pre-slush snows, and I have to admit that even in the city, or perhaps, *because* of the city, I was initiated into a new kind of appreciation for both the season and the surroundings.

Snow in this city is transformative, if only briefly.

It is an afternoon after work, a day of empty ten-to-five to make my rent, and I hop a cab because it snowed afternoon and the streets are already a discouraging brownish grey.

A taxi ride is not a special event, and, like most things in the city, done without too much attention paid to it. The same streets passed on the last ride are passed again, the same storefronts, the same traffic, and so generally my attention is not in any way aroused.

But something about a "snow sky" is different than any other type of sky. The quality of light is different. The clouds are less grey than rain clouds, and so although the sky is overcast, there is a pure lightness of the air, diffused perhaps, or indirect, but pure nonetheless. And as we turn the corner onto my street, still a few avenues away from my apartment, it is that kind of light that hangs amidst the tableau line of snow trees.

And I am struck breathless. From our current corner to as far as I can see toward our destination, both sides of the street are lined with unblemished, untouched, snow-frosted branches that seem to blend into the whiteness of the sky creating a kind of open-weave, stretching, visual archway.

Overall, the streets are empty, void of other traffic or life of any kind, (or maybe I'm so transfixed that I imagine that) and for a moment the curved tree branches adorned with snow are the lace-covered fingers of bridesmaids, interlaced and clasping overhead, ribbons hanging down, making an arched canopy vista for us to swish silently beneath.

It is a fairy tale. A storybook. A dream.

I have never seen this before. Nor have I seen it since.

Indeed, perhaps if I had been a moment sooner, or later, or the sun had been stronger, or the day darker; if I'd had different dreams the night before or woken in a different mood, I may have missed it.

Or, at the very least, it would not have been the same.

This town. Sometimes.

Sometimes it's wonderful.

FLOODING

He thought he had seen the last of it.

The rains.

He thought he had seen the last of the dense, ash-gray skies and rivers of trash careening through the flooded gutters.

But then again --

He thought he had seen the last of a lot of things.

The young boy, for instance, who for so long would regularly set off firecrackers on the corner at hours far past a young boy's bedtime, until the firecrackers took two of his fingers. The screams that night had been like that of the banshee. Cold and eternal. He thought that would have put an end to that. But no, some lessons are never learned. Most, in fact. And the firecrackers exploded again last night, landing in his dreams as a string of nuclear bombs obliterating an already spiritually destroyed, emotionally devastated city.

And then, he woke again to rain.

He remembers, somewhere back in his tired mind, a saying from the Pagan calendar; "If July the first be rainy weather, It will rain for four more weeks together."

Why does he know that? Where would he ever have come across anything even remotely Pagan? And even if he had, why had it remained stored somewhere in otherwise useless brain cells, long forgotten and abandoned only to turn up at some indiscriminate, however appropriate, moment.

Horns are honking. Honking. Honking. He moved to the apartment he now lives in, on a quiet, one-way side street, in the hopes that such intrusions would cease. People use horns in the same way they use most conversation; unnecessary noise produced when all else seems to fail, but which serves nothing in particular save for filling empty air.

And the rain. He'd had a brief encounter with hope when the sun severed its way through a weak point in the cloud cover yesterday afternoon. But by the time evening fell, the clouds had recovered, nursed their wounds and returned stronger for the effort.

He cranes his head against the window, looking first left, then right, knowing he'd see no end to it, but feeling the need to try anyway. Perhaps the same psychology of looking up the tracks for the subway as though that will make it come sooner. Or returning to the refrigerator a half dozen times in the hopes that you missed something the first five, or that some sort of mystical power would have stocked it with something new.

But all he sees are dark, ominous, endless clouds. Clouds so low that if he stood on the roof, he would appear headless.

For the last two days of this unsavory weather he had been struggling with an annoying urge to visit his next door neighbor, Noah, and ask if he had any inside information. In truth, now that he thinks about it, there's been an awful lot of banging and drilling going on next door.

Then again, it's only a studio apartment. More likely he's building a loft.

Below his window stands a homeless man looking like a pile of soggy laundry, ripping open garbage bags in search of redeemable cans. In the process, he tosses every other piece of trash off the curb, where it collects in the growing stream of rainwater and gets washed down the street where it is slowly clogging in the drain on the corner.

He used to like rain. He remembers that suddenly. When was that? He used to like standing in summer showers, laughing at the lot of distraught pedestrians caught unprepared. He'd stand, water streaming off him, plastering his clothes to his body, clinging to his eyelashes, running from his fingertips as though it came from within him. And he'd laugh.

But he was also in love then. And he has long since been done with that nonsense. Thank God he learned that lesson early. Thank God he figured out the game and withdrew himself from the roster before things got really messy.

What was her name? Lorna. Lovely Lorna from California. Yes, he had loved her more than he thought possible. He had mistakenly assumed that the object of love was to be genuine and sincere. To love with every fiber of your being. Lorna quickly corrected his illusion. Quickly straightened out his misconceptions. In a way, he felt he should be thankful to her. Otherwise, he'd still be stumbling around with the same idiotic, idealistic mish-mash blundering around his head. But he's got it straight now. He knows exactly what's what.

He wipes the condensation of his breath off the rain pelted window. He wipes away the disturbing and unwanted thoughts of love and memory. He hadn't thought of her for a long, long time. Didn't think he'd ever think of her again. Thought that was long gone and over with.

Must be all the damn rain. Nothing to do but sit around and let your brain do what it wants. Wander around your psyche digging up all kinds of unwanted garbage. Looking for redeemable cans, but only finding landfill.

"Rain, rain, go away, come again another day."

Well, that's no good. That's precisely the problem. It *did* come another day. It just happened to be the very next one.

What if it never stopped? What if, now that they'd come, the downpours decided they liked the sensation of rushing headlong into sidewalks, umbrellas, rooftops; liked careening down drainpipes and rushing through gutters, decided that was much more exciting than being cooped up in stuffy old clouds all the time playing cards, or bingo, or whatever rain did when it wasn't coming down.

Night. He barely noticed it, having had no sun to compare the darkness to.

He opens his windows as wide as they can go, not caring anymore about the rain throwing itself through the screen. He can't take being so stifled anymore.

He has been thinking about the day his father died. It had been raining then, too. They were sitting watching a baseball game, just the two of them, when an astounding lightning bolt outside the window was followed by a deafening thunderclap in less time than it took to take a breath. His father clutched his chest in that exact moment, his eyes wide like a wild horse with a rope around its neck. He had thought his father was pretending the thunder was a gunshot. As they sometimes did with one another in storms. He waited for the customary "Oh! They got me! The got me!" But it never came. He just drew in a sharp, quick breath as he tried to rise from his armchair, and then collapsed in a heap like an empty bag of bones. Where had his mother been? He couldn't recall.

But there is no thunder with this rain now. Just water. And more water. And the sound of it running off and through the leaves. Is it possible that it is coming down even harder? Is that *possible*?

He listens, trying to answer his question and finds he does not dislike the sound of rain. It was like...like...he could find no words to describe it. He wonders if his lack of dislike meant that he could listen to it for the rest of his life. Could he?

He opens the front door to the apartment building slowly. Slowly, as if the jaws of death awaited him on the other side.

He stands for a moment, in the doorway, smelling the air between the raindrops. Smelling the earth in it. He takes one step out and feels the first drops on his head run down the back of his neck. He feels them on his shoulders.

He takes another step out and finds himself in the middle of it all, gushing over him as he stands in a puddle, his shoes soaking wet, his hair the same.

It drips from his eyelashes and plasters his clothes.

It runs from his fingertips in small rivulets as though it was coming from within him.

It envelopes him, coats him, running tiny rivers around him.

He can't even tell he is crying.

THAT'S NOT WHAT I SAID

He had been carrying on for close to a quarter of an hour, and she, for all practical purposes, had ceased to listen at the half hour mark. She had plenty to do, put the laundry away, wash the dishes that had piled in the sink, clean up the pieces of the mug he had smashed to the floor after the first fifteen minutes, and he didn't seem to really require her undivided attention. In fact, she had the feeling she could leave the apartment altogether and he would continue on quite satisfactorily.

"David -- "

"Ann, do me a favor, just hear me out for once, would you?"

She didn't answer or respond in any way because he wasn't looking at her when he spoke, so if she had made any kind of response he would not have seen it. Instead, she tied the ends of the garbage bag in the kitchen, pulled it out of the container and set it near the door.

"...can you understand that?..." she caught him saying as he sat on the couch hunched over his knees. She began taking dishes out of the drainer and putting them away in the cabinet. She even tried to do it as quietly as possible, despite the fact there was no real conversation going on. She started to put the pots away as well, but they were still wet, so instead, she went into the living room and sat in the chair opposite him, drawing her knees up to her chest.

"David, can I just..."

"Why can't you just listen? You cut me off and of course you don't know what I'm going to say..."

So she watched him, fully involved in the process of saying whatever it was he had been saying for however long he had been saying it. And he was -- involved. Every fiber and aspect of his being had thrown itself completely and totally into the task. His knees swayed back and forth, his hand went repeatedly to his hair, his eyebrows raised and lowered, and his face contorted into an unfathomable number of expressions in the briefest span of time.

She wanted to laugh. She wanted to laugh because when she broke it down into parts that way he really looked very funny. When she broke it down into separate parts, she couldn't remember what he was going on about, and that left him going through all those separate things, all those contortions and fidgets, for no reason at all, and that was funny.

"You think this is funny?" for the first time in nearly an hour he looked at her and caught her thought.

"I didn't say that. In fact -- "

"No. You didn't have to. See, Ann, this is exactly..."

And off he went again. She closed her eyes, letting the sound of his voice melt over her like dripping candle wax; a little painful at first, but entertaining when you peeled it off. But she opened them again because she was afraid the droning sound of it would lull her to sleep and then he'd really have something to yell about. However, he was up off the couch again and standing at the window, back to her, talking to the pigeons on the street lamp on the opposite curb. So she went into the kitchen and dug the one ashtray she had out of the back of a drawer, fished an ancient pack of cigarettes out of her bag and lit one up. He didn't like when she smoked, but she figured he wouldn't notice. She sat at the kitchen table watching the smoke curl toward the ceiling.

"...do you even remember that?..."

She took a long, slow drag off her smoke, watching the end flair fiery red and die down, turning to ash. She held the smoke in her lungs the way she did when she used to smoke pot all those years ago, then let it out slowly in little, perfect rings. Two. Three. Four. She didn't get high anymore, but she wished she had some right now.

He caught her off guard, whirling from the window and throwing his eyeballs in her direction. "Does any of this matter to you? Do you even care?"

"Yes! I care, David. But -- "

"Well, you sure have a funny way of showing it. Are you smoking?"

Before she could take a breath to flatly deny the existence of the dwindling cigarette held in her hand, he let the realization propel him down yet another corridor that somehow pertained to the original point he had been making.

My he had a lot pent up inside him, she thought. The time had now reached an hour and a quarter and she could only recall him pausing for breath twice. She took the final pull on the cigarette and stubbed out, ground it out really, crunching and turning it in the ashtray until the filter was nothing more than a crumpled ball. Then she put a new garbage bag in the kitchen pail, dumped out the ashtray, and returned it to its hiding place in the back of the kitchen drawer.

"So?" he was looking at her. Actually, squarely looking at her from across the room. It startled her. He apparently wanted an actual response.

"So what?"

"You don't have anything to say?"

"Sure I do."

"Well?"

"That's not what I said."

"Oh, that's so typical. I swear to God, Ann, this is why..."

And she watched him begin a small circle of pacing in the living room; on the carpet, off the carpet, on the carpet, off the carpet. She watched him for a few moments, considering him, considering saying something, considering collapsing in a chair and listening some more, considering herself, the apartment, the pigeons across the street.

She went into the bathroom to take a shower.

CAN YOU SEE THE WHALES

It's hard. This city. I live in a tough city in a tough world, and that makes it hard.

Sometimes I love it here. Sometimes New York is life on the brink. It's people struggling to survive, their will, alone, carrying them through. It's energy and intensity, and everything taken to extremes. Sometimes it's the cliché of the dirt and suffering, the grey isolation that inspires and sparks creativity.

But there are times when it is none of that. Times when all I see are empty shells running as fast as they can from point A to point B with no time or inclination to pause a moment along the way. They are too busy making it, buying it, having it, looking like it, to see those that they bump into, run over, or miss entirely. There are times when it is a wasteland of heartless, spiritless bodies who can't see beyond the end of their noses, and their blinders have been on so long they don't even notice them anymore. What's more, if you pointed it out to them, tried to show them everything they've been missing, they'd look at you like you had just fallen out of the sky.

Meanwhile, their eyes are just painted glass.

That's the kind of city it is the day I sit on a bench on the Upper East side promenade of the East river.

Sometimes this promenade is wonderful with the old fashioned street lamps, cobblestone walkway, gulls on the iron rails and the bridges spanning the Hellgate currents.

But not this day. I sit in the sun, hiding behind my sunglasses, music, and headphones keeping me tuned out of their world and tuned into mine. I brood about my lot in this city, and how sad it is that so many people live blind and deaf *without* benefit of shades or earplugs. I look around me at all the people out today; walking, biking, reading. Maybe it is naive and idealistic to think it could be otherwise, but it depresses me to think how those lives will never interconnect. There will always remain a safe distance between them. And therefore, me.

I stretch back against the back of the bench, the sun slipping in the sides of my sunglasses. It makes me squint. How can such a beautiful day fail to fill my heart? That depresses me more.

Across from me, and diagonally down on the other bank stands a lighthouse. I see it when the brief splattering of sunspots clears from my eyes. I remember that lighthouse. I remember the night my boyfriend and I caught a cab to Roosevelt Island after working until four in the morning, where we sat beneath a tree near that lighthouse, the grass wet with pre-dawn dew, and watched the sun rise.

It came up over the bridge of Hellgate, dappling the water little by little. As it skimmed across the ripples, it also panned along the building facades, and like a curtain being pulled up slowly, slowly, it gradually washed everything it touched in a rosy dawn.

Where is that city?

Where is that moment? Lost, I guess.

I turn my attention back to the river. The one that at times is a lulling, peaceful escape, but at the moment is a filth repository and watch the elusive current. I follow a gull as it dives again and again at whatever scraps lay floating just below the surface. Scavengers.

But aren't we all

I am about to follow that same gull back up for another dive when out of the corner of my eye I catch something breaking the surface. I only see it for a second, but it is something very large. I turn toward it, leaning forward slightly to see through the railing and peek over the rim of my glasses that frankly cause more glare than anything else. Gulls skim the surface and pigeons alternately take off and land on the railing, just beyond stands my lighthouse, but the surface of the river remains unbroken.

But only for a moment. Because then, from beneath the surface rises a huge, black tail -- a fluke -- that breaks completely free of the water, waving once, then slapping down *hard*. It appears almost mechanical in its movement, slick, rubber-like black, water falling off the sides like rain. And WHACK! it smacks the water's surface with more power than I'd care to imagine.

"What the hell?" I look behind me to see if the woman there has seen, but she is reading. So I look back to the elderly couple sitting on the next bench, but they are engaged in conversation. Nothing. No one makes any motion to suggest they've seen what I think I saw.

Leaving my seat I go to the railing, my earphones and sunglasses now off, freeing my senses, and I look again. And it comes, a little closer this time, breathtaking power pulling up, up, up, and CRASH! Water spraying high into the air. A whale? That is all I can think of. I've heard of alligators in the sewers, and that was tough enough to swallow, but a whale in the East river? That's impossible! It couldn't fit! Where did it come from? And what's more, where does it think it's going? For a minute I flash on the dolphin that got lost and wandered upriver and died. But then again, I reminded myself that there is no way a whale could fit in New York's East River.

Could it?

Well, I don't have a chance to ponder much further because right in front of me, his blowhole clears the surface and he blows a geyser into the air so high I can feel the spray on my face. Then once again. Pfoof! I am like a child, ranting and raving, screaming.

"Oh my God!! Look at that! There's a goddamn whale in the river!"

On and on I carry. A silly girl jumping and whooping and flailing around. Just when I am ready to accept that as the finale of the magic, just I am about to blink and break the spell, this big old humpback pulls his head up out of the water, and I swear to God he looks right at me. For a minute he just hangs there, and I can see his eye reflecting in the sun. Like crystal. Like a crystal ball that sees everything, knows everything, that holds all the mysteries of the world inside. Big, wise eyes. A chill runs up my spine, through my hair, down my arms. All of a sudden I want to cry. He is so beautiful. So gentle. As wonderful and strange as a being from another planet. And he looks right at me. Right through me. He sees me. All of me. Eye to eye. I can feel him. Sense him. He just wants to say hello.

"Hello."

The tears I can't hold back splatter off the railing, and he dives again, disappearing for a second, rising only once more to blow one more geyser, shattering my tears into a fit of warm laughter.

Hello.

Then he dives again. And I wait. And wait.

But the river remains calm. And inside I feel clear. Happy. Special. I feel the bond of two worlds meshing together, at least for a moment. But a moment so sweet as to last forever.

Then I remember the others. All the people that had been around me, and I can't recall hearing any other voices, any reactions. I was so lost in my own that I never turned to see anyone else. So I do. I can't wait to hear! What a wonderful sight for a street of strangers to share!

But what I meet are not common looks of awe and disbelief, what I meet are shocked faces and frightened children, and the old couple next to me backing warily away.

"What's wrong? Didn't you see that? That was amazing! Didn't you see?" I keep asking over and over, but all anyone does is back away, farther and farther away, and before I know it -- I am alone.

I can't understand. How could they have missed that? Nobody could have missed it.

Unless I imagined it. Unless this topsy-turvy city of insanity has finally taken its toll.

Uncertain I turn back to the rail, staring down at the water and its mesmerizing current. It spins and drifts, rises and falls. Leaves have fallen and are carried bobbing up and down along it. A gentle breeze has begun to stir just slightly, and it caresses my face and hair. The gulls hang magically, paused briefly on a curtain of air before dipping down and diving to the kill. It is beautiful. It is warm. It is home.

I hadn't imagined that. I know that.

They just couldn't see.

Off to my left I hear a muffled "Pfoof!" and I turn just in time to see the spray scatter on the breeze, and the tip of his giant fluke vanish beneath the ripples in the sun.

They just couldn't see.

But I can. I do. And whenever I get lost in the rush and the tumult, whenever my blinders begin to grow, and my heart begins to toughen, it happens --

A fire escape aglow in a streetlight on a summer night. A lighthouse at sunrise. A whale in the East River.

And I see...

MYSTERIES

The Newcomer

I guess you could say I am a woman with a past. I am a woman, and I didn't come from nowhere, so the rest must follow. On more than one occasion I've heard, or rather, *over*heard, myself described that way. "She's a woman with a past." At first, it made me nervous (What do they mean, what are they thinking?), even a little angry (Who are they and what business is it...), but then I thought, well, of course, I have a past. I'm thirty years old and I didn't just appear out of thin air. I mean, everybody has a past. Don't they? Everybody comes from somewhere. Everybody has a past.

People are funny. I think they need to believe in a little mystery. A little malice, even. They need to believe things are more than what they seem, and that often means they need to believe it to be something dangerous. When something they see seems to be more than just what it appears to be on the surface, they almost always assume that what lies below is wild and dark and fascinating. Mysterious. I think people are severely, chronically, fatally, lacking a sense of mystery in their lives and so invent it whenever they find a place it might possibly fit. In this case, that place is me.

I left the life I was leading because it wasn't working and I was unhappy. I couldn't make a living, I was always broke and the city I lived in was cruel and cold and very lonely. I figured if I was going to feel that lonely I would rather it be because I was really alone. And in fact, when I am truly alone is when I feel the *least* lonely. So I moved. I sold everything I had with the intention of a completely new start. It seemed it was a move that had been brewing for a while, one that had been hanging patiently off to the side waiting for my discovery. What few friends I had were either leaving themselves, or I found we were beginning to drift apart. There was no love relationship at the time, so nothing lost there, and my family had been gone for a long, long time. There was only me. And that was ultimately transplantable.

So I chose a quintessential sleepy Southern town on the shore. A place that almost seemed lost in time. A place where everything was reachable on foot, and I could rent a small house for the price of a studio apartment in the city I fled. Quaint. Old. Charming. All the things that the place I left behind was not. However, along with all that, what also went was the possibility for anonymity. In the city, you can be invisible. I suppose everything has a price. Some are just more affordable.

The first time I sensed that inescapable need for mystery was when I signed the lease on my new home. The landlady looked at my name, Sheridan Lansing, and said I must have changed my name, was I an actress or something? I get distracted sometimes, my head fills up with so much that I forget where I am, so it took me a minute to realize she had asked me a question. But when I tried to assure her it was my given name -- my mother loved romance novels -- she pointed to my suitcase and inquired about the initials A.D. on the lock. The explanation that my old best friend Anne Dowling had given it to me when I was in need and she had just been given a whole new set from her boyfriend did not seem to satisfy her. No. She chose to believe that I was hiding something. Something devious or wonderful or dark. Anything other than the simple, uninteresting truth. I found it intriguing and felt bad that I could not fulfill her need for cloak and dagger. What I failed to realize was that I already had.

It happened again when I got the job at the small used bookstore and I filled out all the necessary file information. There, too, they inquired about my name, asking if anyone ever called me Sheri. I replied while browsing a shelf of poetry, "No. Never. It's Sheridan. Just Sheridan." The small woman at the counter seemed displeased with that response as if I was either acting too highbrow for her, or I was leaving something out of the story. Either way, she was incorrect. It's simply that no one has ever called me Sheri, nor do I wish them to. My name is Sheridan. Always has been.

And so the stories began, as they are wont to do in quintessentially sleepy towns, about the new arrival with the fictional sounding name, whose luggage bears other initials, and who keeps to herself a great deal and is (so they assume) loath to answer questions about herself in any great detail. Not that they ever really asked.

She must be hiding something.

Mystery.

I spend the time I am not working strolling along the shoreline. I study the language of the ocean, wishing myself on the sail boats bobbing and drifting so wonderfully far in the distance as they following the gentle curve of the earth, or I perch on logs of driftwood and close my eyes, lulled by the smells, the sounds, all the while aware of the eyes upon me. Waiting for me to slip up and reveal a part of my unknown, unshared past. Sometimes, not often, I miss some of what I left behind. Not much or very deeply, just sometimes, in passing thought.

My favorite time on the shore, though, happens to be a time when few others can be found there. Times when the fog rolls in thick and dense, and light rain dapples the sand and surf. With a light sweater and no umbrella, I carry my sneakers in my hand and walk along the edge of the world, no more than ten or fifteen feet visible all around me. It is like...like I have vanished into a netherworld. Which is all I ever wanted anyway.

Nights I sit on my porch, breathing the sea air, usually with a book in hand. I laugh to myself as passersby toss a quick, unsuccessfully casual glance in my direction and jabber to one another. I think if I was forty or fifty years older, I would simply be eccentric and perhaps even interesting because of it. At the very least, I would be accepted, even if not understood. But somehow, because I am young, and not unattractive (as they say) my choice to be separate, solitary, to live my life in a way not usually accustomed to one of my age, it is looked upon as something that must have a deeper darker reason behind it. I am not eccentric. I am a freak. I am the one they warn their children about. It's sad, really. Although I am not saddened by it. That, too, I'm sure they would find odd.

But I like it here. It is soothing to me. Comforting. I am surrounded by the kind of world that I have always longed for. I go to work, I do my job, I come home, cook dinner, and stand outside at night learning all the constellations I knew as a child but could never see in the city. I am Alice. And I have found my Wonderland.

That I am the only one in it, or who comprehends that, is of no concern to me. I am home.

Landlady

I have lived here all my life. I am not a nosy person by nature. In fact, I subscribe to the notion of live and let live. As long as it isn't going to harm anyone else.

When I first saw Sheridan she almost looked like she belonged to that house. She was sitting on the steps in a long dress almost like my mother used to wear some sixty years ago and a big old wide brimmed hat with lace and flowers. Too big for her if you ask me, hid nearly her whole face. Anyway, I swear, I thought I stepped into a time warp or something. Frankly, it spooked me 'cause for a second I thought she was a ghost. These southern towns with their old houses...well...it's not like it was impossible.

Sheridan just makes people nervous. I mean, when I was showing her the house, I asked her where she was from. She said, "The city", and when I asked her which city, she changed the subject to something about which room gets the most sun, or was heat and hot water included. I can't remember exactly. And the suitcase, well, I'm sorry, but when somebody smiles like she did when I asked her about those initials, you can't tell me that you wouldn't think something was up. Anyway, whatever it was she wasn't saying didn't give me the impression that she was dangerous or anything, and I'm a pretty good judge of character. Have to be if you do what I do, so I rented the place to her. Plus she paid first, last and security without hesitating. Most people hem and haw at least a little. Especially young folk. So who am I to argue? She's got the money to pay, I've got the space to rent. And like I said, when I first saw her sitting there on the steps she looked like she belonged there. So what do I care where she comes from or what she's running from.

But I have to say this -- Sheridan Lansing? That's a made-up name if I ever heard one.

Impressionable Youth

I had seen Sheridan around a lot before I actually got the nerve up to go and talk to her. I don't know why I was so nervous. She didn't make me feel that way. I think it was the stuff I'd heard around. Even my mother told me to be careful. Most of the stuff was just outright crazy. Like there was one story going around that she was a murderess. God! People are such idiots. It never really occurred to me just how backward this town is until I heard some of the ridiculous stuff people were saying about her. I think she's fascinating.

She's always got a book in her hand. Every time I've seen her she's got a different one. Don't get me wrong, it isn't like I follow her around or anything. I'm not a psycho. She's just -- well, she's got a real style about her. Something that makes her different somehow. And I don't know why people say she won't talk. When people do pass by and say hello, she always says hello back with a smile so big you'd think it would hurt her. And she'll ask about peoples' families or businesses like she genuinely cares. Not like she's just making idle conversation. But I watch people. And when her sea-foam green eyes hit hard into theirs, they almost literally take a step back, like she pushed them. And when they start chatting with her without really meaning it, she excuses herself and goes back to her book, or her walk, or whatever it was she was doing. People don't like that.

Actually, I don't know all of this just by watching. I went up to her one day while she was eating lunch and asked her what book she was reading. She showed me, smiling that smile that makes her eyes glow, and invited me to sit down. We talked a while about the book, and I watched how she was when people passed by. Some of them didn't bother to even say hello, they just sort of stared a bit, as if she wouldn't notice, then glanced at me, and went on their way. I was so surprised that it didn't make her mad. It made *me* mad. But she just smiled at their backs as they walked away.

Those eyes of hers are something else. Make you feel she can see right through you.

Neighbors

My wife and I have lived in the house across the street from the one she rented for over twenty years. I admit, she's damn near the prettiest neighbor we've had. Don't tell my wife I said that, she'll board up the front windows.

I see her a lot out front of the house. She's putting in a garden. I remember the first time I saw her I thought it was a fellow for a second 'cause she wears her hair so short, and she had on trousers and a shirt and suspenders like she just jumped out of a gangster movie. Looks kind of sweet on her, though.

Sheridan keeps to herself a lot, which does seem a bit odd to me for someone her age. I'd think she'd be thinking about getting married and having kids. She's about at that time in her life. But they say she's never talked about anyone special, and I've never seen her with anyone around here.

I did see Catherine, Loretta's daughter, stop by the day I saw her planting flowers in her gangster clothes, and they sat on the front steps for a while and talked. Sheridan laughed a lot. She seems to do that real easy. Then she went inside, came back with a book she gave to Catherine, who hugged her before getting back on her bike and heading home. I never said nothing to Loretta 'cause I knew it would get back to my wife and I already told you she'd board up the windows. Besides, Loretta's an old busybody and a worrier and she'd make a big stink because one of the stories going around about Sheridan is that she was having an affair with some girl whose parents had a fit when they found out. It ain't none of my business one way or another, and it sure didn't look like Catherine was in any danger.

I only spoke to her once, and that was in my bakery. I welcomed her to town and told her I thought her name was right pretty, and her eyes were the greenest I've seen in my life. Don't say nothing to my wife though.

Newcomer

I must say that all in all I have grown to truly love it here. I may be something of an oddity here, but they leave me be. There is no reason not to. I think that infuriates some of them. Like I said, they want to believe in something more. I guess some people would wonder why I don't defend myself against it. In truth, I see no reason to. What they assume, or postulate is untrue. I know that. And in the end, that is all that really matters. And I believe, that if I did choose to defend myself, two things would happen. One is that the very fact that I defended myself would lead them to believe the stories were true, otherwise, why would I bother? (The old, "methinks thou dost protest too much" syndrome). The second is that regardless of my defense, they would believe what they chose to believe anyway because they need to. They need their mystery. Who am I to deny them that?

I am not quite as alone as I had expected, or even originally intended to be. I am visited occasionally by a young girl who is very pretty, very smart, and I think views me as a role model for escape into something bigger and grander than her life here. That makes me more nervous than the stories. And I am surprised she hasn't been kept from coming yet. Perhaps it is only a matter of time. It will be sad if that happens. I enjoy her company. She renews my views of life. And I am able to be a child along with her.

The other who prevents me from being totally alone is Maggie. She runs a little bed and breakfast in town that I stopped at once because the building was so beautiful. She took me on a grand tour and told me the whole history. It was the house where she grew up -- she is about my age -- and her parents left it to her and her brother when they died. He wanted to sell it. She didn't. So she bought him out, he went to law school, and she opened a business.

Maggie is red-headed and freckle-faced the way I had always wanted to be when I was a girl. She is eager for conversation and I think somewhat stifled here. She is, I think, more like me than she thinks.

We had dinner together that night after she showed me the house, out on a back porch that looked out over the ocean. I don't have a back porch and I envied her that. I told her so. She said I was welcome to borrow hers anytime I like.

Friend

I love Sheridan. She's funny and smart and has shadows that pass over her eyes the way clouds pass over the sun that I'm sure makes people uncomfortable. But I think that's just because when that happens, they see shadows that they know exist in themselves as well. They ignore them. Sheridan explores them. That's the difference.

Don't laugh, but I love the way she dresses. Like she stepped out of, the thirties, I guess. When I told her that she said she makes a lot of her dresses, and offered to make me one. It made me laugh because in a place where everybody is so stuck on store bought, designer stuff, here comes this blast from the past. And they're beautiful. I asked her once if that was what she used to do -- design -- but she sort of laughed and shook her head. She looked away even. It was the only time I've ever seen anything in her that resembles shyness.

We've become good friends, Sheridan and me. She admired my flower gardens so much -- they go all the way around the house -- I offered to help her plant one. So I'm over there a lot.

And she did make me a dress, right after I helped her plant the first batch of flowers. I really didn't even know her very well yet, but she included a card and signed it, "With much love and fondness, Sheridan". From anybody else, I might have thought it a little strange, but somehow, when you look in Sheridan's eyes you know she just feels those things readily and easily. And simply. It's just the way things are for her. It's just the way she is.

It bothered me when people started commenting on the time we spent together. Like we were doing something wrong by being friends. Like *I* was doing something wrong. Sheridan didn't seem affected, and even said she hoped I wasn't either. I said I wasn't, but it's not entirely true. I just don't get how people can make assumptions like that. They know me well enough to know better, and they don't know her at all. And that's too bad. It's like there's this deep, driven need in them to make something up. Anywhere there's a gap or a hole in their knowledge they can't just leave it be as something they'll never know. They have to fill it in even if they have to invent it themselves.

The scary part is that if they're left alone to invent too much for too long, they forget that it came from inside their own minds and begin to take it for the actual truth.

Sheridan

I watch them, watching me. I am now as intrigued by them as they are by me. As fascinated. I don't think they know how interesting they all are. More interesting than I'll ever be. Because the me they see is made up, but what I see of them is who they really are. They will never know that.

I'm not sure how long I'll stay here. Maybe forever. I don't know. But my flowers are beginning to bloom, and this house feels more like home than anywhere I've ever been in my life, and that's as good a reason as any to stay. I suppose when that's no longer true, I will leave.

Some of those that live here have begun to warm to me. Whether they've decided what they heard was untrue or just unimportant, I'm not certain. It doesn't really matter. Mr. Billings, the baker, gives me fresh cinnamon rolls every time I come in, as long as his wife isn't looking, and Maggie and I take long walks on the beach and talk about wonderful, funny, stupid things. I think she is the best friend I've ever had. Ever will have.

Catherine, my impressionable young friend, has found a boyfriend and doesn't need me much anymore. But she happens by every once in a while to find a good book to read. She tells me she's off to college "up north" next year. I wish her all the best.

I went walking the other day, down a street I'd never explored before, and I saw an old woman on a porch swing in the early twilight hours. Something about her caused me to pause to look at her. She was braiding her long, silver hair, and I hadn't thought she'd seen me until I started to walk away. She called out, "You're Sheridan, aren't you?" I stopped and nodded, and she invited me up to sit with her. She told me wonderful old stories about her youth and her past and how she came to live here when she was not much older than I and had loved it ever since.

She didn't tell me much, but she told me enough. All I really needed to know.

THE WAY IT IS

"Marion!" Ralph bellowed from his seat at the end of the bar. Ralph was old. Older. Old enough. He smoked too many cigars, drank too much scotch and spent far too much time in his seat at the end of the bar.

Marion was younger. Young-ish. She wasn't as old as Ralph, not by a long shot. Which wasn't saying much because almost nobody was as old as Ralph. Or at least as old as he looked. He could've been twenty-five for anybody knew. But he wasn't.

She wiped her hands on a bar towel that used to be green, but was now closer to sludge algae, and meandered over to his seat. She was in no hurry. She didn't need to be. The routine was the same all the time. Every night. The same routine. She knew it well, and so did Ralph. But he seemed to forget that he repeated it every night. Or he just didn't care. But she didn't mind because Ralph kind of reminded her of her father. Her dead father. She had loved him. He drank too much too. But he drank whiskey.

"What's going on, Ralph?" She put one foot up on the ice bin behind the bar and leaned her arms on her knee. She was a stocky woman. What some people might call a "broad". Just above her left elbow on the outside part of her arm was a small tattoo; a heart with a tear. Or maybe it was a drop of blood. It was hard to tell. It was small.

"Not feeling too good, here, Marion." Ralph slurred through cigar smoke.

"You're fine, Ralph. Just had a bit too much I'd say."

"Of what, for chrissake! Every drink I have is watered down so much you might as well give me an empty glass!"

"Now, Ralph, you know that's not true."

"Like hell, it ain't. Where's the owner?"

Again, it was the same thing every night. Like Abbott and Costello. Same questions, same answers, same time, same subject. That's just the way it was.

"I'm the owner, Ralph." She wasn't but it didn't matter because he didn't really care anyway. Or else he forgot what he just asked her. He hadn't taken his eyes from her, but his gaze just returned and looked as though he was pleasantly surprised to see her.

"Hey, Marion."

"Yeah Ralph."

"Gimme another."

"Sure thing."

She took his glass away, dumping the ice in the slop sink, then washed it out and put it on the rack to dry. Then, moving to the opposite end of the bar from Ralph, she took a clean glass, filled it to the top with ice, poured about a finger's

42

worth of scotch and filled the rest with water. She returned and set it in front of him.

"I saw that," he said, puffing a huge cloud of smoke up to the ceiling. A greyish brown mark on the tiles there showed where others had done the same a thousand times.

"You didn't see nothing, Ralph. 'Cept maybe the floor when you fell off the stool."

"Fall off! I didn't fall off!"

"You didn't fall off?"

"No sir!"

"You didn't fall off your stool while I was over there making your drink?"

"NosirIdidnot!"

"Yeah, well, now I *know* you've had enough 'cause you can't even remember falling on your ass!"

Ralph paused a moment in his stupor, suddenly concerned for about a half a second that maybe it was true. "Aah! You're fucking with me, you smart-ass." He leaned back on the stool so hard he tipped it back on its rear legs and nearly went over backward.

"See?" Marion jumped in, "I wasn't lying. I was just having a premonition."

"Prema what?" his cigar was nearly out.

"Nothing. Lemme have a cigar." She reached a hand out to him.

"What! You don't smoke cigars, dammit!"

"I just started. C'mon, gimme one." She flapped her hand in front of her.

"I only got one left."

"Good, that's all I need."

He fished in his pocket, found the cigar and handed it to Marion. She stuck it in her shirt pocket.

"Hey, ain't you gonna smoke it?"

"Nah, savin' it for later." She strolled back to the other end of the bar again, slipped the cigar out of her pocket, snapped it in two and dumped it in the garbage. She started back toward Ralph.

"I saw that." he said.

"You didn't see nothing. You're stewed."

"Am not. Gimme another."

"You didn't finish that one yet."

"It's all ice and water, dammit! Gimme another."

"Not til you finish that one."

"Where's the owner?"

"I'm it."

Ralph puffed on his dead cigar while fishing in his pocket for his other one. The whole bar was empty except for them, and if Ralph would leave, Marion would go home. It was late. But she really didn't mind. She had nowhere special to go. Besides, Ralph reminded her of her father.

Marion propped her foot on the ice bin and took a drink of beer from a glass tucked behind her.

"Hey -- " Ralph squinted toward her.

"What?"

"You drinking beer?"

"No."

"Yes, you are."

"No, I ain't. I told you, Ralph. You're plowed."

"When are you gonna get married, Marion?"

"I told you, Ralph, I'm waitin' for you."

"Get out."

"Really."

"So let's go."

"Can't now, I'm working."

"Yeah, you're full of shit."

"Okay, if you say so. But now don't ask me again."

"No, really."

"What?"

"When are you getting married."

"I like girls, Ralph."

"You ain't no lesbo!"

"Yeah, I am Ralph."

"Get outta here."

"Yup."

"Always the pretty ones."

"That's the way it is."

Ralph chewed on his cigar butt and looked again for the other one.

"Whattaya lookin' for, Ralph?"

"My other cigar."

"You smoked it already."

"Did not."

"Did too. Right after you got up from falling on the floor."

"I fell on the floor?"

"Yup."

"When?"

"Little bit ago."

"Shit."

Marion took another sip of beer. She wished they had a juke box, but the owner was too damn cheap. Ain't that always the way it is.

"Hey, Marion."

"Yeah?"

"What are you doing after work."

"My boyfriend is picking me up."

"I thought you said you liked girls?"

"What?"

"I thought you said you was gay."

"Did not."

"Gimme another."

"You know the rule."

"What rule?"

"Once you fall on the floor you're cut off."

"I didn't fall on the floor, Marion."

"You sure did, Ralph. I had to come over there and help you up."

"Damn."

"Yup."

"Guess I better go. Whatta I owe ya?"

"You paid already, Ralph."

"I did?"

"Yup."

"When?"

"About two seconds ago."

"Did not."

"Don't argue with me, Ralph."

"Okay, Marion." Ralph pushed back his stool and stood up, fishing in his pockets. He pulled out a twenty and pushed it onto the bar to Marion. "That's for you, darling."

"Thanks, Ralph." she was saving up to get out of that town, and she needed a car. "You be careful getting home."

"Always am."

"I know you are."

"See you tomorrow?"

"Nope. I quit tonight."

"You did?"

"Yup. Can't take it no more."

"No."

"Yup."

"That's too bad. I'm gonna miss you, Marion."

"I'll miss you too."

"Yeah?"

"Naw, I was lyin'."

Ralph pulled his coat on, dropped his cigar butt on the floor and shuffled to the door.

"See ya tomorrow, Marion."

"You bet Ralph. See ya tomorrow."

Marion stuffed the twenty dollars in her pocket, downed the rest of the beer in her glass, and made her way to the other side of the bar. She slumped onto a stool and took out a small wad of bills from her shirt pocket. One hundred dollars in all. If it kept going that way she figured five more conversations with Ralph and she'd be kickin' up dust on her way out of town. All they'd be seeing was her tail lights.

Just when she was starting to like the old guy.

Ain't that always the way.

LOVE AND LINOLEUM

Caroline waited for Jack.

She had gotten ready for bed early, primping and preening as though their twenty-five years of marriage were nonexistent and they were about to be together for the first time.

She bathed and perfumed and found a seldom used peignoir, rubbed her shoulders and legs with rose scented cream and then climbed beneath crisp, clean cotton sheets.

And she waited.

She couldn't say it had completely surprised her when he called to say he wouldn't make it home for dinner. She couldn't say it surprised her because she knew he would call. Not because he had said so, but because he had been missing dinner an awful lot lately.

Dining alone had become the norm.

Or not dining at all.

She lit a candle near the bed and glanced at the clock. Nine p.m.

She waited for Jack.

She waited for Jack and remembered that she forgot to call to get an estimate to replace the linoleum in the kitchen. It had been there since they bought the house, but that was over twenty years ago, and now it was outdated. Outdated, worn, faded, stained...old. It was old. And that made her feel old. In fact, she'd like to redo the whole house, but that was entirely out of the question. But a new floor in the kitchen would certainly help matters. Actually, it's amazing what just one small change can do in terms of creating the illusion of something more drastic. That's what she always said. "Just one small change can make all the difference in the world."

One small change.

Just one.

She propped herself up against the pillows behind her and looked in the mirror over the dresser. Wetting her fingers, she smoothed the front of her hair where a stray piece had gotten loose from the style. The faintest hint of grey was beginning to show at her temples. She was actually sort of proud of her grey hair. A sign of experience, she thought. Jack said that if she let it go she would start to look like the bride of Frankenstein.

Her eyes opened. Shit. She had fallen asleep. Not at all what she had planned. Certainly she had smashed her carefully coiffed hair, and although she had hoped it would end up a little crushed, she had not planned on it being from sleep.

The back of her neck was stiff from nodding off sitting up, and her scalp had fallen asleep as well. What a strange sensation she always thought that was. Pins and needles all around the back of her head.

She was about to get up to rearrange herself when she heard the tinkering of dishes coming from the kitchen.

"Jack? Is that you?" she called from her carefully positioned place on the bed.

A brief, halting silence was followed by Jack's voice, "Uh, yeah, honey, it's me."

"Come here, won't you?" she tried in her most come-hither tone.

"In a minute, hon, I've gotta have something to eat. I'm starving."

"Just for a second." she hoped to divert his appetite.

"I just wanna eat and finish up on a little paperwork sweetheart. Why don't you just go to sleep? I'll be there in a bit."

Caroline would have liked to say that this was not the response she had expected. But in truth, it was precisely what she had expected.

That, however, did not diminish the stabbing pain that ripped through her heart. Her hopes joined her hairdo.

She allowed a few moments to pass with only the sounds of the dishes clinking, and water running, and kitchen chairs being pushed and pulled.

She allowed a few moments to pass with no sound at all except for the rapid tremor of her frail heart, and the rhythmic, maddening tick, tick, tick of the alarm clock.

"Jack?"

"Yeah."

"What are you doing? Come to bed."

"In a minute."

"You said that ten minutes ago."

Silence.

"Jack?"

Silence.

"Jack?"

"What!"

Caroline now removed herself from the clean cotton sheets, wrapped herself in her old terry robe, and padded silently down the hall toward the kitchen.

The light spilled out from where he sat, slicing a wedge into the darkness beyond. She stood in the doorway, his back to her at the table, his head leaning on his hands, cigarette smoke billowing up into the stillness.

"I thought you quit smoking, Jack."

"I guess not."

She came around to the side of the table and leaned against the counter staring at him. The coffee cup he drank from had a chip in the rim. That side pointed away from him.

She stared at the chip, counting three more cups in her head that had similar imperfections. Injuries. From use.

"I need to talk to you, Caroline," Jack spoke without raising his head. Just stared into his coffee, and blew smoke.

"I know that."

"I'm not sure how to start."

"I think you do. You must. Because *I* do. Shall I start for you?"

"No."

"Then go ahead." she pulled the terry robe tighter around her not wanting any of the peignoir to show.

"I'm trying."

"No, you aren't, Jack. You are staring at your coffee and blowing smelly cigarette smoke around my kitchen."

"*Your* kitchen?" he looked up to her now, meeting her gaze. A fatal mistake. Because the weakness of it made her stronger.

"Yes. *My* kitchen. You will be leaving, won't you?"

His gaze was pushed back to the coffee.

"Yes."

"That's what I thought. Goodbye."

And she brushed by him, back through the spill of light in the doorway, back down the silent hall, and back into the cool, crisp, clean cotton sheets. Shutting off the light, she slept.

The next morning she woke early.

She could feel it all around her. The missing piece. The loss. The lack. The quiet, strangling tears skulking in corners.

Opening the closet, she pulled all his clothes from the rack and tossed them into a garbage bag. The garbage bag was dragged downstairs and set outside the back door.

The coffee cup still sat on the table along with a note. The note she threw in the garbage. The coffee cup she left on the table.

Opening the cupboard she stared at the remaining coffee cups, realizing there were not three, but actually four more with some sort of chip, or crack or blemish of some kind.

Well, fine. She'd get new linoleum *and* new coffee cups.

Just one small change makes such a difference.

So two small changes should work miracles.

Her tears slipped off the high curve of her cheek without a breath or a sound or a sigh to accompany them. They simply appeared from her eyes as if by magic, leaping from her chin onto the linoleum tiles where they gathered in the small grooves that made up the pattern on the floor and slowly, invisibly, followed the trail of that pattern to the edge and disappeared into the cracks between the tiles.

BOOK TWO

GATSBY II

I want to believe in fairy tales. In magic and make believe. In heroes and happy endings and all things impossible.

I want to. And once in a rare, whimsical while I succeed. For a brief, passing moment I will believe that carousels can come to life, and unicorns with wings will carry me to the other side of the sun. That miracles will happen, and all dreams can come true.

It is a lovely daydream that I always wish could remain just a little while longer. A beautiful daydream too fragile to withstand even the gentlest sigh.

Do you know what I love? Of course you don't. I love the incongruent. I love men's clothes on women. Flowing, antique dresses and combat boots. It is unexpected. But not unpleasant. That is not all I love, but it is one thing. One thing. And chocolate. That is another. I'm sure there are more, but sometimes they escape me.

When I close my eyes, I see an immense garden wound through with stone pathways and littered with finely dressed gentlemen and ladies sipping pale champagne. Cigarettes perch at the end of long-stemmed holders, their burning ends flaring in the twilight like fireflies. Laughter winds through the pathways, rising and falling like the tide, colliding with flower petals causing them to shiver. I am so in love. Is that obvious? I believe I have been my entire life, for I cannot recall it ever being any other way. What a wonder. What a wonder. I believe life should be lived as though we were constantly sitting at the edge of a dock, our feet dangling listlessly in cool, soft waters as the summer sun slowly sets its perfect colors across our upturned faces. I remember.

I think it's sad that people don't write letters anymore. Gone are the days of dimly lit rooms with a crackling fire, a solitary figure at the writing desk penning a correspondence to a dear friend or lover, as the rain trails down the window like shooting stars in the sky.

Now everything is technological. I dislike technology -- it infringes on simplicity. Yes, it is convenient, and may simplify aspects of our lives, but that is not the same as *simplicity*. The motto of the technological age is "DO IT FASTER", but I am nonplussed by that. Why is speed so much of the essence? Can you tell me?

The faster one travels, the less one notices along the way.

Not I -- Words, words, words, my invisible friend! Words are magic. But their poetry is more potent on paper. A pen! A pen! My country for a fountain pen! For monogrammed note paper in palest lilac, scented gently with the fragrance of lavender. Why are we so afraid to be alive! You know we aren't, don't you? Alive. No, no, no. Most of us live our entire lives in a comatose state strikingly similar to that of death.

Does that enrage you?

"Daisy, Daisy, give me your answer true

I'm so crazy, all for the love of you..."

Do you suppose anyone loves that majestically anymore? Or is that possible only in movies and fiction. You probably think I am a child.

Do you know what I think? Do you *want* to know?

I think there was love like that -- *once* -- in the days when one took the time to take pen in hand and caress the paper with carefully chosen thoughts. When time and care had to be taken to communicate with one another. When feelings and emotions were not dirty words to fear. When there was still respect and reverence for the power, passion, and possibility of words.

True compassion and caring are two things left behind in the frantic race of technology.

Is that the price of progress?

I think, then, *I* choose to remain behind.

We are in desperate need of artists and poets and painters, those in love with the gentler aspects of life. They soften the edges of our society.

Are you out there, my silent friend in the darkness? For a brief moment, I could not hear you breathing and thought I was alone. I would ask you to share a smoke with me, but I fear the space between us is too wide. In spite of the closeness we have shared. It's a shame -- I have always believed that little ritual to be bonding. But then, I am a creature of rituals. Not habit, that is different. Once something becomes habitual it no longer requires your presence for existence. Your mind and heart are inconsequential. But ritual -- the simplest ritual performed with truth is a tremendous nourishment to the soul.

I am glad you have stayed. And I know you have. Very, very glad. We don't speak enough of those things, I think, that make us glad. We are quick to point out our frustrations and unhappiness but rarely do we go out of our way to express what warms our hearts. So I take the time now. I am glad.

Have you had enough of me yet? Hah! In truth, I shall never know -- what a wonder! So I must draw my own conclusions, and in that, have no reason not to continue.

I often have the distinct sensation, am quite certain in fact, that I am invisible. I bet you think that's a sad thing, but I assure you it is remarkably pleasant. Like being wrapped in a gauzy shroud. Like being the reader, dear friend, an unknowable specter in the dark, ever-present, ever-watching, but never realized by the characters of which one reads. Or observes. But -- you *know* what that is like, don't you. And how different our Daisy would have been had she been aware of the shadows beyond the page!

Standing on the sidewalk at the foot of the Public Library steps, I feel quite certain that either one or both of the majestic lions are about to heave with life's breath and arch ancient stiffness from their great, concrete bones. How I wish they would! That would certainly startle the surrounding popula-tion out of their carbon monoxide and cement stupor. To see one of *them* breathe one true life's breath would almost be more shocking and inspiring than seeing the same from the lions.   Like watching a loved one emerge from lifelong catatonia.

Strange, don't you think, that they would place such fero-cious predators at the entrance of a building that welcomes one and all to the wealth of knowledge held inside?   And why not something more representative of the place itself? Or is it that being the King, the lion must be wise? Of course, I have forgotten we equate status with wisdom. Don't we? Or is that only age? Ah, wait, I remember now. The one on the left is Patience, the other, Fortitude. Yes, yes. That's right. I remember now.

I stand for a long while, directly between the two immense felines, people cleaving around me like wind around a tree; acknowledging my presence, but not paying it any mind.

What will this place be like in another hundred years, do you suppose?   Will the ornate columns stand crumbling before a once-was building in weak imitation of the ruins of Greece? Will the lions lose their noses or a piece of ear, or perhaps all their paws so they can no longer threaten to rise to life? Will they be our feeble answer to the sphinx?

Turning from the lions and visions of the future, I spy a man selling pretzels on the corner. Steam rises from the grill where he cooks lunches of hot dogs and shish kebabs.   I watch him hand a hot dog buried beneath sauerkraut to a woman with long bleached hair in a Madison Avenue suit of respectable charcoal grey. Daisy would never wear grey. He hesitates just a moment before handing it to her. I think to myself as I watch that he doesn't look like he belongs there. He has the face and stature of a man who is accustomed to wearing a suit and tie. Indeed, he carries himself as though he was wearing one now, as opposed to an apron dappled with mustard and grease.

Perhaps feeling my stare, he glances up at me, catching me in my scrutiny. I should be embarrassed, I suppose, but I am not. He smiles across a greater distance than the space of side-walk between us and holds up a pretzel, offering.

I smile back, shaking my head no.

He shrugs, replacing the pretzel and returning to the business at hand, suddenly looking very at home standing on that corner in his grease-stained apron.

There is always much to learn.

Do you believe me? No, don't answer, it doesn't matter anyway.

How would things change if a law were passed stating that every building in the city had to be painted a different color. Soft, easy, breathless colors of sand and sky and laughter, every building a different shade, no two next to one another the same.

I think it would be like living in a Monet painting, were he ever to paint the city.

I walk for a while along the strange streets of this puzzle, eventually wandering purposefully into the cavernous, cool, silent vacuum of a beautiful, small, wonderfully ornate church on the upper east side. The church of the Holy Trinity.

Instantly I am certain I have gone deaf. It is the one place I have been where the silence is so loud you can hear it. The complete and total lack of sound. The silence is so strong, so dominating I cannot even hear myself breathing. I am nothing. Sweet, perfect nothing.

I feel I have gone back in time. The stone walls and rising wooden beams reach impossibly far into the vault of the ceiling. There is no one there but I. Alone. And yet, there is such an intense sense of fullness.

I am afraid to take a step for fear the sound of my boot on the floor will shatter the very air.

I try to breathe deeper than my lungs, take that silence directly into my body so that I might carry it around with me. So that as long as there is Holly, there is silence.

And I fight a nearly impossible urge to sing at the top of my voice, to listen to the sound being carried up to the peak of the roof, through the timbers, out the steeple to be lost in the blare of horns and screams and smog.

I dream I dream, I dream. I dream often and fully, always in color. Am I dreaming now? Possible. I may have dreamt the whole wretched, wonderful, meaningless thing. But no, I cannot be dreaming, for all I see is black and white.

Sometimes there is a sweetness in the air here. Above the stench of homelessness and despair will rise the sugared breath of early spring.

The fragrance of trees budding in the coaxing sunshine, blossoms revealing their innermost secrets, and the whole of the natural, organic world returning to life. Rebirth. Renew.

It never lasts very long, though. Sad. It leaves me wondering if it had only been a thing remembered from the start. A ghost. An echo. An illusion.

Oh, how I wish to be lifted above the mundane, to transcend the expected and enter a world of whimsy! For some reason, whimsical is reserved for children. That's a shame. After childhood is when we need it most.

CHOCOLATE

Adrianne wasn't positive, although she was certain, nearly without a doubt, that if she didn't have some chocolate soon, she'd most probably kill someone.

There was a knock on her office door. In her mind, she saw a delivery boy with a ten-pound box of truffles and nut clusters. "Yes?"

Gloria, her secretary stuck her bleach blonde, twenty-year-old face in the door. "Jerry asked me to get you. He needs to see you."

"About what? I'm in the middle of something." She rifled through some papers on her desk to locate something she might be in the middle of.

"I don't know. He said it without moving his lips, so I thought it better not to ask the particulars."

"Fine."

Gloria's head receded and the door shut with a click. Adrianne shuffled the papers again and rubbed her temples. Here comes the headache. The tight one that starts at the base of her neck and travels to little pinpoint spots at the inside corners of her eyes; the kind that either make her throw up or turn white. The really good ones do both. She sat a moment, awaiting the arrival of either the nausea or the buzzing in her head. She thought of asking Gloria to run to the candy machine and get her some M&M's. No. She was stronger than that. Enough was enough. When she quit drinking coffee she had a headache for two weeks straight, but she got through it. She could do this too.

The knock came again, and without waiting, Gloria stuck in her head and shoulders this time. "Adrianne, Jerry's about ready to blow, I think -- you okay?"

"Yeah." she shook two aspirin from a bottle, swallowed them, thought again, swallowed two more. "I'm on my way."

Gloria disappeared again and Adrianne thought about what a weasel Jerry was. Long, pointy chin, pointy nose, small, tight eyes. All he was missing were whiskers and a tail. Do weasels have tails? She couldn't remember.

"Excuse me, I'm so sorry to have disturbed you!" the door swung open and shut in one movement sending little sparks across the plane of her eyes.

"Hi Jerry. I was just on my way to see you."

"Really? Must be tough to do while still sitting in your chair."

"Oh please, don't bristle your fur at me. I've got a -- "

"Whatever you have, I bet I have a worse one, so spare me. When I say I need to see you, it usually means right away. Not when you feel -- "

"Hey! Jerry!" Adrianne flew to her feet, knocking the papers littering her desk to the floor, and sending the open aspirin bottle after them, scattering little white tablets all over the carpet. She wished she had a stale chocolate donut to aim at his forehead. "I'll save you some time. Fuck you! Fuck this place! Fuck *you*, did I say that? I quit!"

Jerry, for the first time that Adrianne could recall (although with the pain raging through her temples she could recall very little), looked truly dumbfounded and speechless. She rather liked the expression on him. It complimented his rodent-like features. "What?"

"I'm sorry, I must have spoken Chinese the first time. I lapse into that now and again. I said -- "

"I heard what you said -- "

"Good. I don't like to repeat myself."

And with Jerry standing, cemented in shock, she grabbed her bag, her coat, and a handful of company pens, and the next thing she knew she was on a bus headed uptown. She blinked. Once. Twice. Once more. Something had just happened. Something huge. All she could recount with any certainty was that one minute she was fantasizing about a giant bag of M&M's, and the next minute she had a bagful of TURNER CO. ballpoints that would last her a year. But her headache was gone. And that made her feel that everything must be okay.

Toothpaste. Deodorant. Kleenex. She ran through the list in her mind as she trailed through the aisles of the drugstore. Aspirin. Lots of aspirin. She grabbed two one hundred tablet bottles of Advil. Five hundred milligrams each. Something else. There was something else she couldn't recall. So she wandered through each aisle, figuring she'd know it when she saw it and passed the candy counter. Snickers. Hershey's. Her headache was coming back. A one-pound bag of M&M's. She thought of Gloria. She didn't even say goodbye to her. She liked Gloria.

Suddenly, she wondered how she'd look as a blonde.

Standing in the hair care section she scanned box after box, brand after brand, having no idea where to begin. "New conditioners!" "No peroxide!" Whatever. All she figured was that with her dark brunette coloring she should get the lightest blonde possible to make any kind of difference at all. "Palest blonde." Sounded good. So good, in fact, she forgot all about the snickers bar she'd been eyeing moments before. So good, that when she passed the bakery on the corner, and a man outside offered her a brownie off a silver tray, she said, "No thanks, I quit!" and continued on, proud and strong. But she did take advantage of the red light to pop open one aspirin bottle and swallow two little orange tablets.

Safe inside her little studio in the fashionable east side, she dumped her bag of company pens on the table by the phone. That was when she noticed her answering machine light blinking once, twice, three times. She hit the playback button and went to the refrigerator. She was hungry. Click. Whir. Click. Went the answering machine, and out came the first message.

"Adrianne!" it was a blonde, twenty-year-old voice, "What happened? Good God, I've never seen you like that. Are you okay?" *laughter*, "Jerry stood in your office for ten minutes after you left moving his lips. Call me."

The only things in her refrigerator were milk, muenster cheese, and a bag of Pepperidge farm Orleans cookies. Half gone. She reached for the cookies.

Beep. Click. Beep.

"Adrianne..." the voice of the weasel. She never noticed how nasal his voice was. She wondered if he had adenoid problems. "Adrianne. I think we should discuss the events of this afternoon. I think perhaps you acted impulsively. If you'd like to call me at home this evening..."

She didn't hear the rest because the call of the cookies raged in her ears. She opened the bag. Smelled it. The throbbing in her temples crescendoed in response. And in one, swift movement, she crushed the bag and its contents and sunk it into the garbage pail.

Beep. Click. Beep.

"Hi. Adrianne. It's me. I want to apologize for the other night. I'm not surprised I haven't heard from you, and I've been afraid to call. I got hung up, and it slipped my mind. I know that's no excuse, but, blah, blah, blah, blah..."

Beep. Click. Beep. Click. Click.

Darrel. She thought as she lit a cigarette and turned on the news. What a liar. How stupid did he really think she was? Well, she wasn't calling him back, that's for certain. If he wanted to really make an attempt, he could call her another two or three times first.

She smoked the first cigarette so fast it made her high, and she knew if she smoked another that fast it would make her nauseous and then it wouldn't matter that there was no food in the house. She lit another. Then she went to the bathroom and read the box of hair color. "Shampoo in." Simple enough.

"For maximum color leave in twenty-five minutes, shampoo out." Also simple enough.

She looked at her complexion in the mirror, then back at the picture of the blonde on the box. Then back to the mirror. The picture was smiling huge white teeth, her hair swirling around in a halo. The reflection was not. She tried to imagine the box with her picture on it. She couldn't.

Balancing the cigarette on the edge of the sink, she donned the plastic gloves included in the box and went to work. Being inexperienced she colored specks of the sink, her blouse, and the bathroom rug Palest Blonde as well. Then, she sat on the couch staring at the TV, and thought about the man outside the bakery and wondered how much he would charge to deliver. She checked the clock. In ten minutes she'd give a look.

She only closed her eyes for a moment. She'd gotten a speck of something in one of them, and thought if she closed it and let it water, it would flush out. But when she closed her eyes all she saw were little specks of colored light there in the dark, and the pounding in her temples seemed to drum the rhythm Her-shey's-dark, her-shey's- dark.

She only closed them for a moment, but the clock clearly stated that thirty-five minutes had gone by. She put her hand to her head and came away with a palm full white cream.

"Son of a bitch!"

In the bathroom, she stuck her head under the spigot of the tub, working her hands through the lather until she saw the water begin to run clear. She turban wrapped the towel around her head and made a pot of coffee.

As it brewed the phone rang. She ignored it, allowing the machine to pick up for her, and she listened to Darrel leave another message. She considered fishing the crushed cookies out of the garbage. Beep. Click. Beep. Removing the towel and standing in front of the mirror, she was confronted by a shocking -- but not altogether unpleasant -- vision of a kind of Jewish Madonna. The singer, like-a-virgin, not the real thing.

"Woo hoo! Will you look at me!" And she laughed so hard she had to sit on the bathroom floor. But not without grabbing the hand mirror first so she could look at herself all the way down.

And it wasn't until she had the cut ponytail in her hand and her hair stopped just barely below her ears that she realized she'd had quite an eventful day.

And she was quite sure she had General Foods International coffee, Swiss Mocha flavor stashed in the back of her kitchen cabinet.

WEATHER PATTERNS

The window stood open.

Through it lay the land of wild horses and prairies. Of foothills and snow peaked mountains. A land rich with the cry of the wolf when the moon circled full. Of children all pigtailed and freckled running through sweet summer grasses.

The sheer, white curtains of the Harper's farm house billowed softly. Breathing. Filling out round and full. Emptying. Falling silently along the window frame. Pausing. A lover. Waiting for the invisible breeze. Sails. Tangling edges that rippled, fluttered and fell.

A spider struggled to spin her web in the corner of the frame, the wind tossing her and her silken thread in its breath, but still, she wove, determined to prevail.

The wind rose. Fell. Sometimes pushing through the window, other times just teasingly skimming by while inside, Janine Harper -- of Harper's farm house -- lay drowsy and calm beneath cool, white cotton sheets. White. Snow atop the mountains that she couldn't see from her window, but that she knew were there. Somewhere.

She stretched. Naked skin skimming the smooth sheets, as she carefully eyed the black sky through that window. The usually endless sweep of Montana blue hung heavy and low. Her grandmother's apron full of green beans. The bed sheet tents she made as a child. A woman swollen with new life, a breath away from birth. The prairie grass conceded to the growing strength of the wind, bowing in ripples along the field. The air smelled...alive.

Half in dream, half in bed, she scanned the coming storm. "Steven -- looks like we're in for a big one."

Janine angled her stretch, rolling toward where she knew he lay, Steven Harper. Her love. Wanting the warmth of him to chase away the chill carried on the breeze that blew the curtains.

The bed lay empty.

"Steven?" she half mumbled into the pillow, still more asleep than awake, dimly aware of a quick flash of lightning cutting through the threatening clouds. Far in the distance, beyond the horizon, rain had already begun to fall.

The spider completed another circle around.

The sheets were cold. She drew them close around her, barely aware of her disappointment at finding no one beside her, not awake enough to question. She washed through a partial dream -- giant oak trees cradling her in their arms, tossing her high into the infinite sky where she emerged, splashing, out of a cool, dark lagoon with a waterfall of rainbows and snow...

"Hey sleepy head." Steven's voice pushed through her fog. Wound up through the cold sheets. Skipped over her shoulder, her ear...

"Mmmm..." Was all she could manage in a contented breath as another stretch asserted itself through her muscles, and her eyes struggled to focus on him.

"Are you ready for the storm, Mrs. Harper?" he asked as he slipped onto the bed. Blue and white striped boxer shorts. Two cups of sharp, black coffee. "Seemed like an excellent reason to stay in bed." His lips brushed her ear. Whisper. Corn silk. Memories. Far away the low, guttural rumble of thunder played through the sky.

Janine pulled herself part way up, far enough to accept the mug of coffee without spilling it on the sheets. She took a careful sip, then glanced at Steven. "I could think of a much better reason to stay in bed." She tugged at his boxers. "Get rid of these, would'ya?"

"Not till I have my coffee. And maybe even eat breakfast. I need to re-fortify for chrissake." But he didn't deter her when her hand slid carefully, strongly over him. He felt himself grow hard. He heard Janine moan softly into her coffee. Through the windows, a snap of lightning was followed by a biting crack of thunder. Closer now than moments before. Closer. The wind whistled sharply through the eaves of the house and died away. Whistled. Moaned. Ebbed away.

He maneuvered himself so she leaned against him, her head on his chest, his legs around her, his hardness pushing against her back. They loved to watch the storms. Days they would sit, wrapped in blankets and bed clothes and one another, as the fury outside the window thrashed and raged, seeming at once so far away, and yet born deep within them. The fierce chaos of a storm only served to calm them. Lull them. They loved to watch the storms.

The curtains blew in quickly, snapping. A flag on high mast. The sky flashed brightly and the air cracked again. A baseball hit clear out of the park.

Janine drew his free hand around her, loving its warmth, and she thought...how she loved him. As fiercely as the thunder loved the sky. She thought how if she had nothing else in this life, as long as she had storms and she had Steven, all else was unimportant.

The sound of pebbles striking the windows. The next gush of wind, colder this time. The rain started down. It spilled through the open window, bouncing off the table beneath it, splashing the lace doily and the antique silver brush and mirror that lay there. It threatened to stretch further, reaching for the rumpled quilt on the foot of the bed, but fell short, making it only as far as the edge of the table.

Steven reached for Janine's coffee cup, placing it with his on the table near the bed as he pushed his pelvis into her back, tracing her stomach with his fingers. She laced her hand with his as the clouds swelled further, the thunder ripped the air, and the rain grew to torrents in the wind.

And the spider, nearly finished with her task, was washed away.

She had said something, something she recalled wanting to erase before the last word was spoken. She remembered thinking halfway through it that she should grab the words mid-air and reclaim them. She remembered praying for a bolt of lightning to hit the window, shattering it, obliterating

the words before they reached his ear. But she said them.
And he heard. And now she simply sat, sheet pulled tightly
around her, as if she was suddenly modest or at the very
least, exposed, her knees drawn to her chest, her arms
wrapped around her knees, watching his back as he stood at
the window watching the rain. Rain that had dwindled down
to a soft mist.

"Steven." she barely spoke the word. Afraid that the image
of him at the window was no more than a mirage, a rainbow
after a summer storm, and if she spoke too loud her breath
would send it out the window into the clouds. But it didn't.
And if he heard, he made no motion. He only stood. Blue,
terry robe wrapped tightly. And although she couldn't see,
she knew the muscles of his jaw clenched and released
rhythmically. She knew the words that echoed in his head.

She wished she were a horse. Wild. No thought or
concern, but the wind in her mane. Each muscle propelling
her forward, faster, faster.

She wished he would move. She couldn't see through the
window. Couldn't see what was left of the storm, or the way
the sky had begun to change yet again. Or the way the light
on the field shifted from yellow to green. She wished he
would move so she could see.

The bed was still warm from their body heat in love, and
she cried because all she felt was the chill. The curtains lay
still and lifeless. Framing. Softly. The way she wanted to
touch him. Kiss him.

His shoulders rising and falling. A sigh. His hands
moved to rub his eyes. Were there tears there that he wiped
away? Or maybe only dust that had kicked up in the wind.
Or rain that splattered off the window pane.

Carefully she slid from beneath the sheets, slipping into the shirt tossed on the chair nearby. His shirt. She crept up behind him, slowly, fearfully, so full of love she thought she'd knock him down. The rain had all but vanished, and the clouds, still full and grey, had moved further up into the sky as she reached to touch his hair. "I love you." But he moved away almost before her fingers met the gentle curl at the nape of his neck. Turning away from her. Closing the door to the bathroom behind him. The sound echoing in her ears.

She stood at the window, still streaked with rain, breathing in the smell of rich, wet earth. Breathing in the smell of him in the shirt that covered her body. Breathing in sweetness, sadness, love. Breathing. And the heaviness in the sky lifted. Not much, only enough to allow the first, shy ray of sun to creep through a small crack in the clouds. And that small ray grew stronger, burning off bits of cloud cover, wedging its way through the blackness. Over the rain swept grass and coffee-colored mud. Skimming the edge of the fence. Nicking the peak of the barn. Winding its way toward the farmhouse. Its warm touch finding the open window, where it caught and tangled in her tears.

THE LIFE AND LOSS OF HARVEY LIPPMAN

Harvey Lippman took his job very seriously. When people he met asked him what it was he did for a living he wasn't exactly sure what to say, but he knew he filled out a lot of forms and sent orders down to offices below him and sent and received faxes emails and all of this he treated with the utmost sobriety. He never left early and rechecked everything twice. If they asked for it in duplicate he'd make it triplicate, just in case. He wore a suit and tie, even though others around him carried themselves more casually, especially in warmer weather. The farthest he would go would be to take off his jacket and hang it across the back of his chair. But his shirtsleeves remained buttoned and his tie remained tied.

Harvey wasn't a particularly serious guy in general, he liked to laugh with the best of them and has told some of his co-workers' his all-time favorite jokes. But when it came to his job, he was all business. When it came to his job, his attention was focused and his sense of responsibility high. His job, and his marriage. When he had a marriage. Which he didn't any longer. He did, until very, very recently, but not any longer. He had kids as well, still pretty young, lots of growing up to do, but he pretty much didn't have them anymore either. When the marriage went, so did the kids.

So it wasn't a tremendously big surprise to anyone Harvey worked with when a fax didn't go out, or a number or two was off on an order form. They knew it wasn't that he didn't care about his work because they all knew he took his work very seriously. They all understood that he was under a staggering amount of pressure. As would any man whose wife just up and left with the kids one day, no sign, no call, no forwarding address. And the fact that she did this so very recently, this past week, as a matter of fact, made it all the easier to understand when a phone call went unreturned or the wrong form filled out.

Those kids had been his whole life. His wife too. He had always said he couldn't figure out why a beautiful woman like her would want an average guy like him and didn't he hit the jackpot. Well, it seemed a beautiful woman like her *didn't* want an average guy like him. Not for an entire lifetime anyway. So he threw himself even further into his work. But that only made matters worse because he was so distracted all the time that things kept going wrong, so he spent long hours and days submerged in things gone awry and repeating the same task over and over until he got it right, which only served to increase the frustration and reinforce the reasons he'd made up as to why she might have done what she did.

"Hey Harv, you gonna get that?"

"What?" he looked up from a stack of empty forms to see Jack pointing to his phone. Jack was married with one kid who he coached in little league on the weekends. Jack didn't take his job very seriously.

"You're phone. It's ringing."

"Oh." Harvey picked it up and after a few seconds realized he had to say hello. He did. Then for a moment, he forgot who it was he had called, then remembered they had called him, and so he said hello again. But all he heard was the click of a line disconnecting and then a dial tone. He couldn't remember what it was he had been doing and then recalled the phone in his hand but had no idea who it might have been that he was supposed to be calling. He hung up, figuring if it was important, he'd remember.

That afternoon when he'd missed a meeting because he was staring at his name on a business card trying to figure out why the letters seemed scrambled, they suggested maybe he should go home and get some rest. He'd been under a great deal of stress, they said. Maybe even take a few days off, they said. So he straightened his tie, put on his jacket, picked up his briefcase and headed for the bus stop.

Midtown at midday was a bustle of busy worker bees, and he wondered where they all could be going in such a frantic and important rush. All of their lives couldn't be as crucial as they all made it appear. Could they? On the corner of Fiftieth Street and Seventh Avenue, one short block from his office, he wanted to walk to Sixth Avenue to get the uptown bus home, but for an instant, he couldn't recall which direction that was. He stood there, briefcase swinging as he turned in circles, feeling quite certain that if his heart pounded any harder it would surely explode from his chest. Well, at least then it wouldn't matter which way Sixth Avenue was. It seemed a hundred lifetimes that he stood there until the awnings and shops and delis around him began to look familiar and he remembered which way to go. One block east and the bus stop was on the corner.

He took a seat in the back where only two others sat. One a young man with earphones in his ear, head bobbing and swaying, and a woman in a smart spring suit, her ashen hair pulled back into a loose ponytail, her manicured nails holding the paper open in front of her. She looked familiar to him. She looked... She looked...

He looked away. He'd rather look at the street bums and drunks who didn't remind him of anything. He envied them sometimes, like now. Envied their oblivion. He'd rather watch the streets outside the window, like watching TV, so he could just let his mind blank out. Wander. He didn't want to have to think or feel anything. He wanted to sleep.

When he opened his eyes, he had that momentary panic of not knowing for certain where he was or how he got there. In that panic, he signaled for the bus to stop and he leapt out the door and onto the street before he was even sure he wanted to. Behind him, he kept hearing someone shout "Mister, mister!" but he hadn't known anyone on the bus so it couldn't be for him. He glanced at his hands as the bus pulled away. They were empty and he couldn't shake the strange feeling that they shouldn't be. Wasn't there something in them when he had boarded the bus? Maybe not. If it was important, he'd remember.

He walked until it was nearly dark, over to the park and then back west again, all the while searching his pocket for his house keys. They weren't there. Then he'd think that it didn't matter because Susan would be home, or if not her, Teri or John, and... Then somehow he knew that wasn't right. But he didn't want to think too long on why that was so.

Back at the park again he sat down on a bench, watching the streetlights come on up and down the avenue. He was hot and tired and could feel the sweat begin to drip down the center of his back. He ran a finger around his collar line, but never once, not even for a second, considered taking off his jacket and loosening his tie. People there seemed to have urgent places to go as well. He tried to think of where that could be and why he didn't feel as urgent as they all looked. The work day was over, they were probably heading...home...

Suddenly he was so tired. More tired than he thought he had been in his entire life. He would've gone home, but he was certain it was quite far away, and he didn't have his keys anyway. Things seemed to be just about as bad as they could get. But he didn't want to think about that now. So without thinking much at all, he lifted his feet up on the bench and lay with his head on the other end, and with his hands as a sort of pillow, he let his eyes close. In the morning, things would seem better.

In the morning he would go to the office and turn in the reports he had been working on so diligently before his life was so rudely interrupted.

And just before he drifted off to the gentle swoosh of evening traffic he did a mental check as to the whereabouts of those reports and got a very clear picture of his briefcase sitting on the back seat of the bus he had taken uptown.

He wondered if his children missed him and if his wife maybe had just lost her mind for a moment. It wasn't out of the question. It has been known to happen. He reminded himself to check on that in the morning.

In the morning.

In the morning things would...

In the morning things...

In the morning...

Harvey Lippman fell asleep on a park bench on Central Park South as his wife pulled over just across the Pennsylvania state line, leaned her head on the steering wheel, and cried as softly as she could so she wouldn't wake the children.

In the morning, she thought, things will be better.

ASTROIDS, AMBULANCES, AND ANGELS

Harold had lived in the same apartment with his wife Sandra for fifteen years. For fifteen years he heard the sirens scream by their window on their way to the hospital across the street. The wailing, howling lilt coming from miles away growing louder and louder, impossibly louder as it reached their window and made the turn around the opposite corner. Anywhere you lived in that city you would hear sirens. They just heard it louder, and more often. It didn't even mean anything anymore, except that they had to turn the TV up a moment or pause in their conversations. It never occurred to them anymore that it meant someone was hurt or dying, or dead. It was just another sound. Like truck brakes, or impatient horns, or squeals of teenagers that often sounded like they were being strangled.

"Harold, I think I'll go down to the market today. I'd like to get basil and chamomile." Sandra poured herself another cup of coffee and curled up in the armchair.

"Okay." Harold wiped a piece of soot that had flown in the window out of his eye and then turned the page of the paper.

"Feel like taking the walk with me?"

"Maybe. Let me know when you're ready to go."

They had never had children. Not that they didn't want them, it just never seemed to happen. Now Sandra was over forty and it didn't seem to her like it was going to happen. It didn't usually bother her, only now and then when her mind was empty of all other thoughts, she would wistfully turn to wondering... They were happy, she and Harold, rarely fought, still loved the simple things of one another, and were one of the few remaining couples they knew who were still married. She thought Harold would make a terrific father. She wasn't sure, in spite of her fierce love of children, if she would make as good a mother. She didn't know what Harold thought.

"Hey, " Harold peeked over the paper, "did you see this -- "

He was cut off by the shrill shriek of a siren rounding the corner, screaming for the right of way in spite of a red light. He didn't really hear it, didn't pay it any mind at all. In fact, his pause in speaking was more like an unconscious, Pavlovian response to the sound. Sandra teased him that he would even stop snoring in his sleep if one went by.

"What?" Sandra resumed after the ambulance left.

"This thing about the asteroids on a collision course with Jupiter?"

"Yes! Aren't there six of them?"

"Six pieces, I think, yes."

"Just shows you -- "

"What?" Harold said with a smile, knowing his wife was about to offer a bit of her wisdom.

"Just that there's so much we don't know, can't predict, and will never be prepared for. Life is precious, my love, so I think you should come to the market with me."

She smiled endearingly in that way that always made her look about sixteen and peaches and cream. That was when she most looked like the person she was always compared to, Audrey Hepburn. He laughed, loving the way, no matter what the subject, she could turn it into a testimonial as to the shortness of life and our need to embrace each and every moment of it. Sandra wore crystals and spoke of reincarnation. Harold ate red meat and hoped that when you died, that was it. Period. End of story. Because he knew when he died, he'd be tired of the whole damn thing.

"Will you be mad at me if I just hang around here?"

She leaned over him and kissed him softly. "Absolutely. But you can make it up to me later." She moved to get her sunglasses and keys from the table by the door. "I don't suppose I could convince you to fix the kitchen faucet while you're just hanging around here?"

"Hmmm...That is something that could be arranged."

She blew him a kiss and closed the door behind her. Harold was constantly amazed at his luck at winning her. If he believed in a divine presence, he would say they were destined for one another. Sandra had always insisted that her guardian angel had led her straight to him. Perhaps. Sandra was the dreamer, and Harold the skeptic. That was one reason why he was so fascinated by the fact that they ended up together.

Getting up from the couch, he poured himself another cup of coffee. Sandra had left the milk out on the counter and he silently chided her for it. As he moved to return the carton to the refrigerator he distinctly heard Sandra call out his name.

"Harold!"

It was a loud burst of sound seemingly right in his ear, as though she was standing on his shoulder. It was so piercing and commanding and completely unexpected that a tremor raced through his heart.

Leaving the kitchen, he returned to the couch where he prepared to set his coffee cup down on the end table. He returned to his reading but felt uneasy, unable to concentrate. His stomach was upset. He decided to forego the coffee, and moved to pick up the cup and bring it to the sink.

At that exact moment, a siren erupted into the air. The same siren they heard all the time, every day, and never truly noticed. But this one seemed to blast within his own head, and the coffee in his cup spilled over the side onto the article about the asteroids. The blood ran from his face and he broke out in a cold sweat.

The hospital was right across the street. He was at the emergency room door when they pulled up, and he caught her gaze briefly before her eyes closed and they rushed her inside.

She was unconscious when they finally let him see her, but she would be fine. A taxi cab jumped the curb. Another woman was knocked down, but only after the cab had plowed past Sandra. He sat quietly with her, holding her hand, incredibly unconcerned about her recovery. He just knew. She'd be alright.

Late into the night her eyes fluttered open and found him sitting beside her.

"Hey..." he whispered to her.

"You knew..." she sighed.

"What?"

"You knew, didn't you?" she was groggy and not speaking very clearly, but Harold understood her perfectly. Whether he wanted to admit it or not.

"Yes." and as she smiled at him then, with that infamous smile, he held her hand tightly in his. "I knew."

Outside her window, closed against the night air, a siren howled in the late night. The sound of it wafted past them, up beyond the highest skyscraper, farther out into the infinite blackness where it bounced off the stars and plummeting asteroids and joined in a choir of angels.

DEATH AND THE MATRON

"Gladiolus and lemongrass." The old woman replied in answer to my question about what she most remembered about finding her husband dead in his study.

"I'm sorry?" I paused in my note taking, uncertain she had heard me correctly. For an instant, I thought I was witness to her initial stages of senility.

"Gladiolus and lemongrass." She turned and looked at me for the first time in a while, retrieving her stare from out the window beyond which lay her Monet-like gardens. My next thought was that she was referring to something outside, perhaps wanting to change the subject. Perhaps choosing not to return to that particular place and time. I was about to question that when she clarified for me. "That is what I most remember."

"Gladiolus and lemongrass?" What struck me so about this old woman was her childlike voice. Time had taken its unashamed toll on her physically -- she appeared to be little more than paper maché -- but her mind, and her voice with its wind chime laughter had escaped the time passage unscathed.

I was doing an article on her late husband to accompany the retrospective of his work next month at the Whitney. She had become a bit of a Garbo-esque figure since his death, and I was not certain why she had consented to an interview with me now. Not that I had any intention of inquiring.

"Yes." She went on, "It was that time of year. The gladioli were in full bloom, and the breeze through the study window picked up its scent with just a slight undertone of the lemongrass." She trilled a laugh into the sunshine that bathed her through the window. Me, it left in darkness. The sunshine, not the laughter. "I remember how delighted I was at the way it perfumed the whole room. I wished I could catch it and hold it until the stuffy days of winter."

This was not at all the answer I expected. Indeed, I had labored for days over what questions to ask, and whether or not to ask the difficult ones, and if I did, exactly how to phrase them. Their life together had been a long, close, happy one, and I did not look forward to opening any painful wounds.

Instead, I seemed to have sparked delightful memories.

She looked at me inquisitively, apparently bewildered by my confused silence. Then she laughed again and reached a frail hand out to the table to retrieve a glass of iced tea that sat there. "Does that shock you?"

"Shock me?" Suddenly I had lost all sense and knowledge of how to string more than two words together at a time.

"Yes. That that is my strongest memory of that moment."

"Actually, I guess, no. It doesn't. Not shock, exactly."

"That's good. Because it shouldn't. Memories are a very strange thing. It is not that I do not recall the shock and disbelief, or the rage and fear, or the sadness and grief. Oh yes, all those things are quite clearly, eternally, burned here, " she used the hand not holding the iced tea to lay over her heart, the knuckles gnarled and bent and paradoxically delicate, "but if what you want to know is what my *strongest* memory was...Well, it was that potent and unexpected fragrance. I guess that somehow, the perfume in the air was even more unexpected than finding him dead."

Her last statement seemed to strike something in her. A thought she had never had before. She sipped her iced tea and turned her gaze back to the window. In her serene movement, I was reminded of an owl.

I struggled with myself for a moment, knowing I was there to ask about her husband, but suddenly finding myself much more curious about this woman.

There were none of her husband's works on the walls of the room in which we sat. There were photos of him though. Alone and with her. On the piano, on the mantle, on the table near her iced tea. They had been very much in love.

"Do you play the piano?" I asked her since the door to the keys was raised, leaving them exposed. Waiting.

"Oh dear lord no! He was the creative one in every way." Again the chiming laugh up the scale and back again. "Well, I could play a pretty mean chopsticks."

We shared a laugh together. It was a stunningly profound moment in its lightness. Inconsequential, and yet I would never find a way to thank her for it.

The afternoon had grown comfortably warm, and with the heat came a rising mix of scents. Powder, lineament, and just a gentle whisper of lilac. A whisper that would swell momentarily if a breeze blew in through the window. She would breathe deeply each time it did, as though it was that very scent that sustained her life.

I had intended to ask a few brief, pertinent questions about her husband and their life together and then bid her a fond thank you and leave. I had intended a short, simple meeting, professional and complete, and to be back in the city before dinner. But something had changed the moment I sat down with her, and now I found myself communing out on her front porch as the afternoon began to slowly slip behind us. She sat on the porch swing, her frail legs looking like they should snap in two each time she gave a little push backward.

"We lived in the city when we were first married." She glanced toward me, "It was different then, you know."

"I'm sure it was." My notebook sat closed at my feet. I had stopped taking notes hours ago.

"I don't think you can even imagine. It was good for us then. Especially for him. But, after a while, we realized our souls were in desperate need of the natural world. We were starving for a sense of the basic, real, simplicity of life. Well, at least *my* soul was. I think he was happy just about anywhere. He saw something special -- whether beautiful, desperate, innocent or horrific -- in just about everything."

It was strange listening to her speak of him as though she were vastly different from him when in fact, the things she said of him seemed to me to be the perfect descriptions of her. I wondered if she knew that. I wondered if she knew she was as much an artist as he was.

"Have you ever painted, yourself?"

"Me? No, I told you, he was the creative one. Although I dabbled in poetry, had a few things published in magazines."

"Really?" I was surprised. I'd never heard anything about that.

"Mm-hmm." She sent the swing back in a gentle arc and looked at a point in the sky that somehow I couldn't see.

"How come I don't know any of them?"

Her eyes closed as she rocked, "I told you, he was the creative one."

There was no resentment in her voice, no emotion one way or the other. She simply stated it as fact as though it had nothing to do with her whatsoever.

"Does that bother you?"

"Bother me?" Her eyes flew open and looked at me with the sincere, wondrous curiosity of a child witness to the birth of a butterfly.

"Well, yes, that you never got any recognition..."

It was fascinating to watch her mind work in her eyes. She truly rolled my question around as though she had never considered it. In fact, watching her then I became quite certain she never had.

"No." She answered simply.

What was suddenly very funny to me, was that I began to feel very sad. Sad that I was sitting with a remarkable, gentle, funny woman who had gone virtually unrecognized save for her relationship to her husband. A treasure in her own right, the proverbial perfect pearl, hidden behind a blinding pile of diamonds and rubies, but there nonetheless. And I was reminded of how many undiscovered jewels lay strewn about the world, all in unassumingly plain view.

But why was I saddened by it if she was not?

Why did it rake over a raw part of my soul and leave me feeling somehow responsible for a terrible wrong?

"What's on your mind, child?" She asked me unexpectedly. Child. Such a strange thing to be called once you are in your thirties. What is more, I was unaccustomed to answering questions. More comfortable asking them.

"Nothing. I was only thinking."

"That's what I asked you." She smiled, lighting up her eyes as though she were an actor stepping into her light. Eyes the color of the moon reflected off still, calm waters.

"I was thinking that I wish I had met you sooner." I nearly choked on the words, unexpected emotion rising foolishly in my throat.

"Sooner than what?"

"Than now. I -- I just..." Again, I felt at an embarrassing loss for words.

"I can't understand why. You're here now. Wouldn't gain much more by having done it sooner."

She made me laugh. In spite of my confusing rush of dark emotion, she forced a short, but sincere laugh from my lips, and then leaned back, pleased at her accomplishment. As pleased as if she had just put the finishing touch on her own Sistine Chapel.

We sat in silence for a while, I not having any immediate questions, she, content on the porch swing, and simply listened to the evening begin. Crickets started slowly, one joined by another, then answered by two more. A light breeze skimmed the willow draped near the corner of the house sending a silent shudder through its tendril arms.

There was a tremendous sense of peace there. In that time and space. And there was no doubt in my mind that it had less to do with the gardens and the silence, and the gentle winds than it did with the unerringly honest, simple woman sweetly rocking, rocking, rocking in the early dusk.

Without looking I knew quite suddenly that she was soundlessly weeping. There was no clue from her, no drawing of breath, or shuddered sigh. But I knew because the light changed around us, and the crickets had ceased in their incessant creaking. I knew because the swing had stopped rocking, hanging still, so still in the twilight.

I moved from my chair and sat beside her on the swing, not looking at her, just sitting beside her.

"You miss him very much, don't you?" I asked almost without speaking.

An impossibly deep breath took all the air around us into her lungs, and her voice came out smaller than I'd heard it so far. "Oh...can you smell that?" Her hand came to rest over mine. I paused, uncertain how to answer. Uncertain what she meant. Her hand squeezed mine gently as a single tear trailing down her cheek reflected the gentle glow of twilight. "Gladiolus..." She whispered. "Gladiolus...and Lemongrass."

The most difficult moment of my entire life to date was the moment I kissed her powdered cheek and said goodbye.

The most difficult thing I had ever done was to leave that place behind.

I had found something there, something I had no idea I was looking for. I had traveled farther than the hour and a half drive outside the city. And it was an even longer way back.

It nearly broke my heart -- I could feel it straining within me -- to turn my back on her world and get in my car because

I knew it was the last time I'd ever see her. I knew that as certain as she knew she smelled the gladiolus.

And all the way back to the city the scent of lilacs filled my car as though it was growing all around me.

In fact, I believe it was.

BOOK THREE

GATSBY III

I do not ask for much in this world, and yet what I do request remains elusive. I do not ask for fame and fortune, nor to be surrounded by things exorbitant and unnecessary. I do not, I suppose, pursue quantity, but rather, quality. And yet, it is the quantity which seems ever-present and prized, while quality remains a ghost in the fog. Or worse, a leper shunned and scoffed.

I have been on this earth long enough not to be surprised by that, and yet I am. Forever surprised. Forever bewildered as though I've been told that blue and yellow make pink even though I know they make green.

Ah, no matter. These are all just drops in a bucket. A spit in the wind. There is only one thing of importance. And that is life. Just life. That's all.

There is a place in Central Park, I cannot recall the name of it, but it is a place so firmly embedded in the trees and pathways that no buildings can be seen. One can almost believe they are in the country woods of New England, or perhaps if one is willing and desires, the mystical woodlands of Camelot. There is even a brook that, pardon my cliché, babbles down a gentle slope, tumbling over moss covered rocks and slipping beneath a small, brief, wooden foot bridge.

I nearly expect to see the gnarled nose of a troll in the bushes or feel the fluttering wings of a fairy on my cheek as I sit on a bench in the patch of sun between two maple trees. My book is open on my lap, my head bowed toward the pages, yet my mind wanders to the chirping sparrows and the seemingly forever-courting pigeons cooing and purring behind me.

A girl of perhaps five years old erupts in a fit of bubble giggles as she runs past my bench after two such pigeons. They flutter into the air, tangle around themselves and light again a short distance from her. Her long, blonde curls twine around the sunlight like tendrils of fire as she explodes again, chasing them over the grass and into the air. "Mommy, mommy, look!" And she stops abruptly, turning in my direction, apparently expecting to find her mother there. But there is no one there but myself. Instantly the lovely bubbles of laughter dissolve into pools of glassy tears, disappearing precisely as if they'd been popped by a pin. Moving toward her I kneel in the grass at her side.

"Are you lost?" I ask her, gazing straight into large brown pools.

She says nothing, rubbing her tear streaked cheek, her eyes falling to a small crystal pendant around my neck. The sun catches in it and it flares rainbows against her face.

Not aware that her tears have stopped, she reaches one impossibly tiny, lost finger toward me, gently touching the crystal. Rainbows dance.

"Do you like it?"

Without moving her gaze from the pendant, she nods.

Taking her hand, I lead her back to the bench and wipe away her tears.

"A long time ago, when I was a little girl about five years old --" her eyes flick to mine in recognition, then back to the pendant as I reach behind my neck and undo the clasp, "this was given to me by a woman who saw me one day when I was very, very sad." I hold the pendant in my palm now, in the slant of sun between us. "She told me it was a magic crystal that would keep me safe, and that with it on I didn't need to be scared, or sad, or lonely."

The girl watches me closely now, tears nearly forgotten.

"She told me that one day, I would meet a little girl who needed it more than me, and I would know this little girl because when she touched the crystal it would send rainbows into the air." Again the flash of recognition in her eyes. Eyes that grew wide with the unspoken thought, 'Me?'. "And she said that when that day came, I should give it to that little girl because I no longer needed it."

With that, I hold the necklace out toward her, reaching behind her as she leans forward, and secure the clasp around her neck. It hangs beautifully, innocently against her, shining and singing with sunlight as it never had on me.

"And one day, " I brush the last tear stain from her face, "you, too, will meet a little girl, and you will know it is time to pass it on to her. Yes?"

Silently she nods as a smile as bright as the sun on her hair bursts across her shy face.

"Now -- let's go find your mommy." Taking her by the hand I am about to guide her off the bench as her mother, frantic and pale, comes around the curve of the path.

"Mommy!" She runs from my side and into her mother's arms. Her mother looks to me and smiles a thank you over her child's shoulder. I smile in return and move to retrieve my book from the bench.

Instantly the child is off again, running down the path after pigeons, gushing laughter and rainbows, yelling "Goodbyyyye!" over her shoulder into the sunshine and trees.

Oh, how resilient they are. Does she even recall the frightened, panicked tears of moments before? No. For she now wears the magic pendant. A small trinket with rainbows locked inside. A talisman with the power to work miracles in the eyes of a child.

And, in truth, in mine.

I have a lovely word for you. Austere. It is a beautiful, haunting, poignant word, and so full of its meaning as the sound of it rises on a breath deep from your lungs that I find it difficult to believe you will be the same person once you have truly listened to yourself speak it aloud. Impossible? Ah, you forget how often I speak of the power of words.

Power.

The skeletal latticework of trees against a white winter sky; Austere. The look in an old woman's eyes as she gazes out at the river at something no one else can see; Austere. A crisp, autumn twilight seen from the rooftop shadows; Austere.

Austere. Austere. It is not spoken, it is exhaled. It is born. It is an echo.

I think, perhaps, the difference between myself and the masses is that I live *in* things, others live around them. I live in words, paintings, music. I live in sounds, light, moods. Someone laughs, I am in it. Piano keys trill, I am in it. Smoke blackens the sky, I am in it. Do you see? The difference? Oh, I am nearly strangled by the desire to share it with you! Nearly suffocating with it. In it. IN it. It is the difference between knowing the lake water is cool because you strolled the banks and were occasionally splashed by the wake of a passing boat, and knowing its coolness because you ran off the edge of the dock and leapt in. Do you see? In it.

I am intrigued by you, out there beyond my reach. Shadows dancing around me. But shadows are always intriguing, aren't they? We think we see all kinds of things in them. Devils and angels, monsters, ghoulies and nothing at all. So I suppose my interest in you is not surprising. As shadows, you can be anything I imagine. Is that bothersome? For it means I could imagine you incorrectly. I could imagine you simple and plain when you may be impossibly complex. I could imagine you a God when you may be merely mortal. I may imagine you exceptional, when you may be ordinary. My mind is my world and there I am free to create as I please. But then again, the same goes for you. I think, perhaps, you forget that at times. But, that is why I am here. To remind you. Well, now that is a lie. It is not why I am here. But I shall remind you anyway.

I look around and am surrounded by towering monoliths of steel and cement, great, cold, unemotional monuments to nothingness. One would think it would create tremendous claustrophobia, and I suppose for some it does. But not for me. Shall I tell you why? Because in my mind, I see great rolling plains and distant mountains. The wind whipping down the avenue as it is caught between the monoliths is the sweet breeze running through prairie grass. It is, at least, when it is not simply the wind trapped in the man-made caverns of the city struggling, like so many others, for a way out.

I say, "Let them eat cake!" What does that actually mean? Do you know? Because to be honest, and I believe I should be as much as possible without giving too much away, I do not think I do. Know. What it means.

Ah! No matter, because what I meant to say was -- gardens. Let us plant gardens! Every four blocks, the fifth for a garden. Flower garden, vegetable garden, corn, sunflowers, roses. Herbs, orange trees, and peach. Oh, yes! Picture it! Picture it along with the buildings painted the colors of Monet and I guarantee it will be a vastly different place. It will be a real life Still Life. A three-dimensional creation lifted from the canvas. Monet's flower gardens. Van Gogh's sunflowers. Who did vegetables? Did anyone? Well, perhaps I shall, and then they can be Buchannan's vegetables! There really are endless possibilities, you know. But, like the power of words, we have forgotten the strength of imagination. But, I remind you -- as I am wont to do -- there, inside the vast nothingness and blackness within ourselves, lies...everything.

Ah, there is so much, so much, so much, and time so brief. And yet, every once in a while I turn around, and there is nothing at all.

What could be more wondrous?

LAUNDRY NIGHT

It is Tuesday night. And every Tuesday night I drag my bag of laundry down the street to Suds and Spin for a rollicking evening of wash and dry. Tuesday night is my night off from Billy's Tavern, where I pour beer and shots for an already drunk crowd until three a.m. while country bands wail and moan and twang about broken hearts, cheatin' spouses, and a life-gone-nowhere. Actually, Monday is my night off too, but I am usually too tired all day to think of doing anything besides sitting in my pajamas and watching daytime TV, so the laundry falls to Tuesday. I have thought of doing it during the day before I go to work since my shift doesn't start until four in the afternoon, but that's when all the housewives with their screaming kids are there and the wait for machines is almost the whole afternoon anyway. So I come on Tuesday nights with all the other lonely hearts, when the place is nearly empty.

I load my stuff in the washer, pump in the quarters, and leave my box of soap on top of the machine. I sit on a chair right in front of the machine and start to read the book I brought with me, but that lasts all of about three seconds because it's so unbearably hot I think I'll explode, so I go outside to the bench by the front door instead. It isn't a whole lot better, it got hot fast this year, but at least there's a little bit of a breeze that stirs up every now and then and cools the sweat from the last ten minutes.

I get through about two paragraphs when I get this funny feeling about something inside, so I turn and look in the window. There're only three other people in there; a girl about the same age as me in a trashy tank top you can just about see through staring at the dryer going around, a nice clean-cut guy of the suit-wearing variety cleaning his horn-rimmed glasses, and an old man sleeping with his head tipped back and his mouth hanging open who I think isn't even doing any laundry. That's when I notice my box of soap is missing from the top of the machine. Maybe somebody borrowed it. That's okay, but it would be nice if they just stuck their head out the door and asked first. More likely, though, somebody swiped it. They'll steal that old geezer's dentures if he's not careful. Goddamn assholes. I just bought that box too. I consider marching in there and conducting a brutal interrogation, but it's just too damn hot and I'm not up for a lot of flying accusations and denials over a box of Tide. If they're that desperate, or their clothes are that dirty, let them have it. I can't be bothered. It takes enough energy just to sit still enough so you don't sweat to death. I can't be bothered with expending any more energy than that. Still, it burns me. Stealing somebody's box of soap. Especially when you pick it up and find out it's almost full so you know they just bought it.

"Hey, Karen, what's up?"

I look up to see Jeremy across the street waving, but not stopping.

"Hey Jer, what's doin'?"

"You going to Trina's this weekend?" he almost drops his bag of groceries and stumbles in his attempt to catch them.

"Maybe. I haven't decided."

"It's gonna be great. Always is. See ya!"

"See ya."

Every year Trina Horner has the first party of the summer in the little courtyard behind her apartment. Trina and I don't really get along, although we are friends and have been for a couple of years. It isn't that we don't like each other really, we're just very different. Trina's older than me and afraid her biological clock is going to tick her into oblivion before she has a chance to procreate. So she basically spends most of her time looking for, thinking about, talking about, and sizing up -- Men. It gets tiresome, and so although I think she's generally a good person, I can't spend more than two minutes with her without wanting to smack her. This weekend is her party. I'll probably go.

The sun goes down far enough for the streetlights to flick on, and I can hear their dull hum in the quiet of the early evening. Somewhere down the street, I can hear the tinny sound of a stereo through an open window. I cock my head slightly in an attempt to identify it, and I think I do a couple of times, but I can't be sure because it really isn't loud enough. I check my watch. The clean cut guy with the glasses tromps out the door with his bag of clean laundry and I catch his eye briefly before he goes the other way up the street. Did he take my detergent? Creep.

I go back to my book again as a breeze kicks up for about a half a second, teasing, before disappearing down the street. The streetlights are on full now, and early evening has settled in. It's almost quiet except for the tinny music and the occasional exchange of curses between Mr. and Mrs. Carmine on the corner. I can hear them through an open window too. It's hot. Everybody has their windows open. I try for a while to hear what they might be screaming about this time, and that's when I see the car turn the corner to my right, only slowing down a little as it passes in front of the Suds and Spin and I hear the clatter of trash cans across the street. I didn't think it had jumped the curb at all, so I couldn't imagine what had caused such a racket. Then it squeals tires just a little as it skids off down my street and turns the corner again at the end. When I look back, this jumble of clothes detangles itself from the overturned garbage cans and stands half in and half out of the streetlight. He runs his hands through his hair, pushing it back out of his eyes and turns to face the bench where I sit.

"Hi. How ya' doin'?" he gives a sort of half wave that matches the half smile on his half charming face in a boyish sort of way.

"I'm fine. I think the question is, how are *you*?"

"Me? I'm great. Great."

I just look at him, my eyes narrowing.

"Oh, that? Hey, they were in a hurry, I had to get out here, I told them not to bother to stop, I'd just jump out."

"Into the trash cans."

"I misjudged a little."

"I guess so."

He starts across the street toward me and I keep thinking I should be very nervous about this, but there's something about the way he walks, a little stooped, a little tentative, and the way his wolfish eyes are surrounded by that little boy smile that makes me just sit and wait for him to reach the bench and sit down. He does.

"Are you okay?" I ask him.

"Yup. Fine. Trash cans broke my fall." he smiles, and those wolf eyes sparkle. He runs his hands through his hair again, which I can see now is a light, dusty brown and had been greased back before he fell out of the speeding car. He had about a day's worth of growth on his face and was wearing a once white t-shirt, jeans, and cowboy boots cracked and soiled with age. I imagine he's worn those boots across country and back again.

We hear the squeal of tires again, and he stiffens at the sound, turning quite suddenly, grabbing me in his arms and kissing me, pulling my body across in front of his. I suppose I should have fought this, imagining a hail of bullets raining through me on their way to him, but he's a damn good kisser, and he isn't hurting anybody, so I figured, what the hell?

When it's quiet again, he sits back looking a little sheepish, which I find endearing, and says, "Sorry. I thought for a second..."

"That's okay. Any way I can be of help." It is a stupid thing to say, but I'm not feeling particularly bright. He is an excellent kisser.

"My name's Jimmy." he holds out his hand, which is remarkable clean, and I shake it.

"Hi. Karen."

"Nice to meet you Karen." he looks me up and down now, and I try to imagine what he sees besides a girl with hair shorter than his, an ankle length summer dress and cowboy boots.

"You too."

"So what are you doing here, sitting on a bench by yourself?"

I point to the sign above our heads, "My laundry."

"You live around here?" he doesn't look at me when he talks now, but glances nervously around him, watching corners and traffic, and passersby. Occasionally he catches my eye, relaxes for about a half a second and smiles.

"Uh-huh. Sort of. You?"

"No. Other side of town." he fishes a cigarette out of his back pocket and lights up. "Want one?"

"No thanks. So what are you doing in my neighborhood?"

"Taking a ride."

He says it lightheartedly enough, but I'd like to pursue it the way I wanted to find out who took my detergent -- that still burns me -- but I can be bothered with it about as much, too. So I leave it hanging there, wondering if he wanted me to ask him more about it. He looks sort of disappointed.

"So, Jimmy, what are you going to do for the rest of the evening?"

"Oh, I don't know, " he takes a long drag off his cigarette, "I'm just gonna sit here for a while if you don't mind too much."

"Nope. It's a free country."

We sit in near silence for a while and I try to go back to reading, but I can't because he's sitting so close to me, his boot butted up against mine and I feel like I should be saying something to him. Being that he just fell out of a car and all. But I can't think of anything to say, so I just sit, pretending to read, listening to him drag on his cigarette, wondering how long he's going to sit there.

After a while, I realize I haven't looked at my watch for a long time, and my wash is probably waiting for the dryer if someone hasn't stolen it yet, and when I turn to look in the window I notice the girl is gone and I don't remember seeing her leave.

"Hey, I have to go put my laundry in the dryer. I'll be right back."

"Go ahead."

I get up and go back inside, assaulted by the stuffy, hot air and all the fans broken, and I want to get my stuff in the dryer and get back out as soon as possible. I keep thinking that Jimmy is kind of cute, and if I'd met him under different circumstances, I might even ask him out. But all in all, I don't like the fact that the first time I saw him, he was climbing out from under a pile of garbage cans.

I glance out the window as I put my stuff in the dryer and see him stand up and stretch his arms over his head. He's lit another cigarette and starts to pace a little in front of the bench. I get the impression he is trying very hard not to turn and look inside the Laundromat.

I go back to my laundry, transferring the last of it from the washer and pop in my quarters, wondering what Jimmy was going to do next. I actually thought of inviting him to Trina's party. First I laughed at myself, and then thought, why the hell not? He doesn't seem dangerous. In fact, he seems a little scared. I bet he got mixed up in something that he had no notion of until it was too late and now he just wants out.

He seems like a pretty decent guy all in all. Even though he is a little jumpy. But I'd be jumpy too if I just got let out of a car without it stopping first.

I make sure the dryer is working okay, watching the clothes for a few spins, then turn to pick up my book and go outside. The book isn't there. For a second I turn on the old guy still asleep with his mouth open, but then I remember I left it outside.

I bounce out the door to the bench only to find it empty, Jimmy gone, and with him, my book. Down at the corner, I hear what sounds like a can being kicked, and I think maybe he just got restless and took a walk, although I don't know why he'd take my book with him. I run down to the corner, "Hey!" I yell into the empty darkness. There is nothing. No one. I go back to the Suds and Spin, seeing Mr. Carmine slam out his front door and head down the street.

I sit down, a little pissed at first, both at the fact that he left before I could invite him to Trina's and that he took my book with him. I was almost finished with it. Now I'd have to buy a new one. That and laundry detergent.

Then I sit for a while, the drone of the dryer audible through the door, the night cooling a little as it wears on, and I remember something. My name and address are on the inside cover of the book. He could return it if he wanted.

PIGEONS

It all happened quite suddenly. Or, perhaps it happened unsee-ably slowly, year after year after year, and was only noticed, only coalesced in that quite-suddenly instant.

It was the first true spring day of the year, in spite of the fact that the calendar had marked the beginning of spring a good two and a half weeks ago. It was the first day that people walked the streets with their jackets slung over their arm and laughed with their faces turned upward toward the sun rather than hunkered toward the pavement against the grey wind. Summer hopefuls dotted the curbs, suds buckets at their feet, sponges soaping down winter-scarred cars while the can of wax waited patiently on the front seat. Windows were thrown open, the brown, heavy air trapped inside since last October being sucked out in the sudden release to be replaced by blue skies and crisp sunlight falling over sofas, carpets, and lazy, sleeping cats.

She slept in. She shouldn't have, really, but that's the way it turned out and it felt so good that she didn't concern herself with it for very long. In fact, even after she woke she lay in bed a long while, the sun draping itself over her like an electric blanket, pillow scrunched into a ball beneath her head. The only thing holding complete perfection at bay was the absence of the aroma of freshly brewed coffee. Had she taken her first morning's breath with the rich, warm smell of hot coffee in the air the whole rest of the day would have been a bonus.

She had things to do. Mundane but necessary errands that she had put off because it was always cold or raining or both and she preferred to remain inside. But this first true day of spring encouraged her, enlivened her, and even the mundane business felt light and acceptable. So she had set out to do them, just a few simple errands, while the sun warmed her remaining winter chill. She took a moment on the front stoop to allow the easiness of the day wash over her. One would think she was standing atop a hill in a mountain meadow, the scent of pine and heather tickling her nose.

Perhaps she was.

Mental checklist: bank, post office, drug store, bookstore.

She zigzagged across the blocks to always walk in the slant of sunshine, shying away from the deeply shaded sidewalks. They reminded her of winter, cold and long and bitter. She thought instead of lying down on plush green grass and staring up at the empty blueness of the sky. Of red wing black birds and swans gliding through serene ponds surrounded by cattails, and rabbits hip-hopping through clover. Clover. When was the last time she lay in clover?

Reaching a corner, she chose to wait for the walk sign across the avenue rather than crossing the street into the shade, even though she had to go there eventually. Wasn't that always the way? One more block in the sunshine was worth the wait of a red light. Her gaze fell unfocused before her toward the opposite curb. A gust of wind kidnapped a discarded piece of newspaper. The paper grabbed a hold of a rear view mirror, clinging for dear life, but in the end, the gust won, sending it first high into the air like reverse confetti, and then finally flinging it hard into the gutter. It lay still. Lifeless.

The sun felt somehow brighter for a moment, like a flashbulb, and that was when she saw them. The shadows of an immense flock of pigeons as they collectively leapt from their perch on the eave of the bank across the street, circling wide through the intersection and settling on a ledge behind her. Shadows that seemed three dimensional, like little blue angels swimming through the cement, dappling her as they flew overhead. Then, just as they settled, just as the last bird touched down, they'd take off again, following the same swooping path back to their original perch. It was as though they were playing a game. Red light, green light, there on the corner in the first spring sunshine. She couldn't figure out why the light hadn't changed. Every time she glanced at the sign it said DON'T WALK in glaring red. And then the pigeons would fly, confetti shadows falling across her again, raining over her. When they settled, she again prepared to cross the street, to complete her errands, but the sign wouldn't let her. So she stood, waiting, waiting, and the pigeons would again take to the sky, back across to the opposite side, and it was this wonderful, orchestral thunder in her ears, and she felt sure that if there were just a few more they would block out the sun in their flight like a fleeting heartbeat of an eclipse. They were a tornado around her, a tempest, an aerial waterfall of birds and their shadows. With each pass, the vortex intensified, like a whirlpool of which she was the center, and suddenly, she stopped looking for the WALK sign. She just stood, waiting for the next flurry of shadows, for that gentle, lovely rush of animated ink spots across the pavement, for the roar of their collective wing beats and heartbeats, not caring if she ever got across the road. Not caring if she remained there until the following winter moved in, as long as the sun shone and the pigeons cascaded their shadows around her. She swore she could even hear them laughing.

AFTERNOON TEA

She moves to sit at the same corner window table in the same square of midday sun that she sits in every afternoon at the Peacock Cafe. She gets as far as grabbing the back of the iron chair to pull it away from the table so she can slide in when something tells her it is wrong. Or, not wrong, so much, as too ordinary. Too much the same. Every day, once the weather turns, she comes to this cafe and sits in the same chair at the same table and orders the same thing; Jasmine tea with a slice of lemon.

Well, not this time.

Indeed, the sun is hitting a much better table to her left, and hitting it in such a way that she could sit in its glow but still be angled to see both out the window, and the surrounding tables as well.

It sends a small, rippling thrill through her as she takes her new seat at the new table. A little excitement of veering slightly off the beaten path. The waiter passes, noticing her choice, raises his eyebrows and smiles. She dips her head, somehow embarrassed as if it was a very private act she had just performed. Perhaps it was.

Sliding into the chair, one closer to the wall and therefore a snug fit, her skin seems sensitized. Her dress sliding and twisting slightly around her legs as she maneuvers on the seat feels cool and silky and deliberate.

The waiter comes by to take her order, and when she opens her mouth, flirting with the idea of altering that as well, she falters, suddenly shy and uncertain. "Jasmine tea, please," she says.

"With lemon, yes?" the waiter replies.

She nods without looking at him, ashamed at being so timid, unhappy that she is so predictable.

She opens the book she has brought with her, her notebook lying closed and waiting nearby. Thoughts hit her occasionally, sometimes overpowering and unavoidable, and she jots them down so they won't distract her. She opens the book, holding it flat between clasped hands as she rests her arms on the table and gazes out the window. The sun is strong today, and the warmth is lulling and enticing. She feels it soak into her skin and run down through the length of her body. She closes her eyes.

A darkness passes over the light through her eyelids, an eclipse of her reverie, and she opens her eyes to see a silhouette hunched near the window in front of her. A figure on the sidewalk scanning the menu. The figure moves, the sun returns, and for a moment she is blinded by it.

"Here you go." the waiter appears with her tea and lemon.

"Thank you."

The waiter surreptitiously walks away and she sighs, thankful he didn't try to engage her in any sort of dialogue.

Turning to her open book she reads the same sentence four times before she realizes she is, for some reason distracted. Pausing, she explores this distraction, examines it, wonders if it is from within or without, and finally concludes that she is sensing a presence that was not there when she first walked in.

Glancing up toward the other tables she sees a man seated, facing the opposite direction from her; had he been at her table he would have been seated directly across from her. Something strikes her as familiar, in a vague, dreamlike way.

The silhouette of moments before. He had been the eclipse peering at the menu.

It is curious that he has caught her attention. He is not particularly imposing in any way. Not overly tall, or built, or dark. His hair is a dusty brown, falling somewhat unkempt to just past his collar, and he wears slightly oval horn-rimmed glasses. His jaw is not noticeably squared, nor is his nose particularly angular, instead his face as a whole has a softness, in an inviting sort of way, and the way he is hunched over the book he reads, one hand propped against his cheek captivates her. She is magnetized. He raises his head for only a moment, to acknowledge and thank the waiter who has brought him a steaming cappuccino, and she knows she is risking being noticed in her stare, and yet she cannot seem to break. She revels in the half smile he flashes as he says thank you, and how he uses his left thumb to twirl the ring he wears on the ring finger of the same hand.

Her heart races within her, and her lips have gone dry. She thinks to take a sip of tea to rehydrate, but she is afraid to look away. He is a mirage, dependent on her stare. Her hands are clasped tightly now, and she releases them only long enough to pull the elastic out of her hair so that it falls freely. The ponytail had begun to feel tight.

He reaches for his cup without looking up from his book, bringing it slowly, slowly, to his lips, sipping carefully through the foamed milk, and setting it back in its place with only a quick glance at the table.

She remains motionless, a deer in the brush, praying he doesn't look up, praying he doesn't sense that he is being watched, wanting only to see him. Look at him, uninterrupted.

She swallows. He turns the page, sighing full and deep, and she exhales quickly as his shoulders rise and fall. She imagines his lungs filling deeply, fully, and then pushing out again in a gentle stream of breath. Her hair falls forward, and she runs her hands through it to push it back, the feel of the strands through her fingers wild and soft. Her fingers tingle.

He turns a page, sips his coffee and spins his ring completely unaware of her persistent stare. He turns and drinks and spins as she feels her entire body splitting apart, atoms and neurons and bits of herself decomposing and falling away, melting into the sunlight through the window. Her teeth are buzzing and her head feels swollen and the line between her body and the chair has all but completely vanished. And all he does is sit and read, spinning his ring, with his hair a little askew and his small, tight arms holding open the paperback book, his eyes soaking in the words, his brain their meaning, and he will never know.

She sits, melting away, not really even staring at him anymore, only toward him, as he closes his book, and pays his check. Outside, his shadow passes between her and the sun only briefly, flickering, as the waiter clears his table and then comes over to her's.

"Anything else?" he asks.

She knows he wants to ask about the faint smile she feels emerging. A smile born of somewhere just below her center and revealed only in the slight curving of the corners of her mouth.

"No thank you. Just the check." And she reminds herself to order the orange spice tomorrow.

ACCIDENT OF BIRTH
(or, Intentions Gone Astray)

She hadn't intended it to be anything more than something simple and innocent. She hadn't intended it to escalate and when it did, she hadn't intended on it going as far as it had.

She hadn't intended anything that had happened, but she had also learned by the time her thirtieth year rolled around, that intentions very rarely had anything at all to do with what actually occurred. People spent a good portion of their lives uttering the words, "Well, it isn't what I intended" in regards to one thing or another. Sometimes it is good fortune such as when an artist says, "Well, it isn't what I originally intended, but when I saw what it created, I thought..." and other times, it is not such good fortune, as in, "I never intended to sleep with her..." Intentions or the lack thereof come in many shapes and sizes, and as already stated, the actual events of life rarely fall in accordance with what we intended.

And so Jackie Herald finds herself in the position she is now in, because indeed, and quite honestly, this was not in any way what she had intended.

"So, he's meeting me after work." Jackie checked outside the office door again to be sure no one had entered the restaurant and was waiting to be seated. There was not. She let the door close quietly and checked her reflection in the mirror. Still there.

"You're kidding!" Kelly's voice over the phone indicated clearly that her eyes blew wide open and her right hand slapped her thigh.

"Nope. I just sort of walked by the bar, asked what he was doing after work, he said nothing, and I asked him out for a drink." She returned an errant strand of hair to its proper place. Out of her eye.

"I am so completely shocked."

"Tell me about it."

"That is so not like you."

"Tell me about it." Jackie thought of his smile as he laughed with customers at the bar and tried to identify the plummeting sensation in her stomach. She wiped her palms on her jeans. "Kelly, I gotta go."

"Call me."

"Will do."

Jackie had never intended to ask him out at all. In fact, when she had first seen him several years ago, she thought he was a little too confident in himself. He was a flirt. And a good one at that. Too confident, she thought.

Funny. That's what she likes about him now.

Three beers later, and not quite alone at a bar, but acting like they were, she thought about what a good time she was having. Not that she hadn't expected to, but she didn't think she would laugh quite this much, or have this much to say, or want to stay as long as she already had.

"How did you get so beautiful?" She heard him ask her.

"Accident of birth." She heard herself answer.

And suddenly she was afraid to keep staring at him the way she was, but even so, was more afraid to look away. She should be going, she hadn't meant to stay out so late.

He walked her out the door to the corner to get a cab. The bar was closing.

"I had fun, " he said, " I didn't expect to stay out so long."

"Me neither."

When the evening had begun, although she wondered what it might be like, she had no intention of anything more than a simple, quick kiss of thanks and plans to maybe do it again sometime. It certainly had not been her intention to be leaning against a building on the corner, making out like teenagers for an hour and a half as the sun began to rise, and the traffic picked up, and the owner of the bar locked up, and newspapers were dropped, and homeless asked for change, and cars honked, pigeons woke, coffee brewed and all the while him, saying, "Where the hell did you come from?" and her not knowing what to say because she already used the Accident of Birth line, and she didn't think it really fit here anyway.

She hadn't meant for her knees to buckle when their lips met, or her heart to stop when he pulled back again to search her eyes, to connect with her in that deep, unspoken way, or her stomach to drop every time he spoke her name.

And as he peeled himself from her, disentangling their fingers and convinced her to get into the cab, as she pulled away, glancing once out the back window at his bewildered figure on the corner, she thought again about intentions. Why do we have them if they rarely pan out as -- intended? Are they there just as preliminary guidelines, or springboards for actual, realized events? Or are they one of life's funny little ironies, giving us a reason to sit in cabs at seven in the morning with no sleep, no desire for it, sweaty hands, trembling heart, thinking, "Well, *that* was certainly not what I intended."

Indeed, it was not what she had intended.

Just a half hour later, as she sat with her coffee, the sun up full, suits and high heels on their way to begin their lives, her phone rang.

"Hello?" Jackie answered.

"Hi." he replied, "Just wanted to make sure you got home okay."

Her breath caught, and she knocked her coffee over sending the spill across the table to drip off the other side. It was an accident.

IT was an accident; the whole thing was an accident. This stuttering heartbeat, caught breath, thrilled-for-a-phone-call feeling.

It's not what she intended.

But here it was.

She smiled.

DO NOT ENTER

I may not know a lot of things -- in fact, I don't. But I know that kids love to run fast, and it can pour with rain while the sun is out, and I know that lonely is a much bigger word than the number of letters it takes to spell it.

I live with my mother on a street with a Do Not Enter sign on the corner. My mother is old, and although I love her, it is often like living alone. Except without the privacy.

The street is a quiet one because of that sign, sometimes so quiet -- especially at night -- I'm not sure that there's anyone else alive except me and momma. If you can count her. Sometimes I'm not so sure.

Every once in a while somebody steals that sign, and traffic gets confused and noisy until someone else comes by and puts up a new one. A couple weeks later it's gone again.

You know, even though I say that living with momma is like living alone, I really can't imagine what it would be like to be without her. She is who I make breakfast for, and do the wash for. She may not always answer, she may not always know that I am there, but it is someone to say "Hello, I'm home" to when I come home from work.

Sometimes people tell me to get a dog, it wouldn't be as much trouble and you get the same reward. I understand what they mean, but I don't agree.

I don't have to take momma out for a walk in the middle of winter.

Actually, that's not entirely true. I do have to load her up once in a while and push her around for some fresh air. But I love her, you know? She's my mother. And sometimes I look at her and think that I see me in forty years and that scares me. Those are the times that I think I can actually feel my skin sagging and wrinkling off my face, and my bones curling and growing soft, and I have to run to the mirror to remind myself of who I am.

My mother was beautiful when she was young. Had her pick of any boy in town. That's what she always used to tell me. But the first time she saw my father, she knew he was the one. But she made sure he worked for it all the same.

Daddy died five years ago. I think she misses him. I think she's trying her hardest to get to where he is. There are times, late at night, when I can't sleep and I'm sitting by the window, listening to nothing, and suddenly I am at her bedside, leaning close to see if she's still breathing. She always is. But sometimes I have dreams that she isn't.

Sometimes I think about packing a suitcase and disappearing before she wakes up in the morning, tiptoeing down to the street before the first light of day. I don't have any idea where I would go. But then I feel bad that I think things like that, and I'll get up the next morning and make her favorite breakfast. Fruit Loops with peach slices and skim milk.

The days I like the best is when momma thinks I'm her sister, Tara, and that we're back in the house where she grew up. She'll chatter on all day then, about things I don't have any idea about. But as long as I nod and laugh with her, she'll go on all day and night, and it's so nice to hear her voice, I try my best to be who she thinks I am.

The street sign is back up again. I never see anyone take it down or put it up. It's almost like it does it all by itself. Like it does its job for a while, then takes a little vacation. I've even tried to catch whoever it is in the act, peeking down the street at about the time it should disappear, but I could sit all night and not see a thing. Then the next night would go by and I'd forget, and the next morning -- it's gone.

"It's the damndest thing," my mother would say if she had a mind to. "One of life's little curiosities." That's what she use to call me, too. One of life's little curiosities. She hasn't said that in a while, though.

I wonder sometimes what it is like to be her, sitting around all day, eating Fruit Loops, not saying anything. Then I realize, I know what it's like because I do pretty much the same thing. Just for different reasons.

ONCE UPON A TIME

On this day Katherine Anne Morrow sits in a peach colored wingback chair at the second-floor window, her hand gently enclosed over a monogrammed lace handkerchief.

On this day Katherine Anne Morrow sits, her gaze distant and intent, with only one, single thing on her quiet mind.

Her life.

Ninety-three years ago to this very day, on May first, nineteen hundred and one, Miss Katherine Anne Morrow came into this world.

She came into this world, and into the very townhouse in which she still lives, kept in her family in spite of pressure from a growing metropolis to sell it for renovation into an apartment building.

Ninety-three years old, and she can recall her childhood of so long ago as if it had occurred this very morning. Just a few, short hours ago.

She would lie on the carpet in the parlor downstairs and stare at the vaulting ceiling, following its curved, bay front around until it made her dizzy. She would fix her gaze on the chandelier, its ornate base hiding silent faces and flowers. She would lie on the floor, knocking the toes of her shiny, black, buckle shoes together, click, click, click, like the constant rhythm of the grandfather clock in the front hall.

It was a difficult home for a child to grow up in, everything so priceless and fragile and in need of great care. Too many carpets for young feet to trip on. Too much china to be broken in the fall.

So she would lie on her back, making no sound or motion save for the clicking of her shoes and stare at the pristine white ceiling rising so far overhead. And she would listen to the clinking of tea cups in the air above her as her mother entertained afternoon guests, laughter and chatter circling around over her head.

Click, click, click. She would wait for the faces in the chandelier to come to life. Click, click, click. Until her mother would retrieve her and whisk her away from the flurry of women and into her room for a nap. Her mother would sit, so tight and upright in her corseted dress, and read her a story that always began, "Once upon a time, a long time ago..."

Once upon a time, a long time ago...

Strange, she thinks now, shifting the lace hankie to the other hand, she could now use that phrase to begin the story of her life.

Once upon a time.

Indeed, she feels she has lived more than long enough. Seen the world change in ways she never would have imagined. Amazed that she hasn't run screaming in terror from it all long ago.

Long time ago...

Retrieving her tea from the table beside her, she blows lightly across its surface and sips carefully.

There, in that room, time has barely passed a day, save for her reflection in the mirror. And even there, the eyes she sees are the same eyes that spent countless afternoons gazing up at the ceiling.

It is beyond the window that so much has moved passed her. So far beyond she can scarcely comprehend. Nor does she wish to. The telephone rings at some point in the afternoon, her daughter Melanie wishing her a happy birthday and letting her know she would be arriving that evening with her own daughter, Chelsea.

For a long time, Katherine Anne had been worried that the time of her townhouse had passed, her daughter having no interest in taking possession when the time came.

But, in the strange cycle of generations, Chelsea has picked up where Melanie chose not to go and has made it clear that she looks forward to living out her days in the same house, in the same way Katherine Anne has. In fact, one of the matters they need to discuss this visit is Chelsea's suggestion that she move in soon; to share the gifts of that home with her grandmother.

Katherine Anne smiles, imagining her granddaughter another sixty years down the road, drifting from room to room, collecting the memories of her own past.

But she finds it difficult to picture the house that far down the line. She fears that its time in this world is very limited now. It is, in truth, special to only two people now. Katherine Anne, and Chelsea. Perhaps they are the last.

Finishing her tea, Katherine Anne leaves the cup and saucer on the side table and moves to the hall and down the stairs to the front room.

The immense French doors, as always, stand open, the marble fireplace visible opposite. She glances at the sofa and pictures of her mother there, pouring the tea, forever the gracious hostess in a vastly different time. No one comes to tea anymore.

Standing there, in the center of the room, she can very nearly hear silver spoons pinging against china cups, and the soft trill of her mother's laughter as she rises to answer the doorbell.

No one has a doorbell anymore either. Not in this city.

She considers using the lace hankie to wipe away the single tear that has appeared down her left cheek but decides she rather likes the feel of it. In it, is carried all the memories of her life.

Glancing at the grandfather clock, she sees that her daughter and granddaughter will be arriving in less than an hour. As much as she looks forward to their visit, she almost wishes she could remain alone. There is something special in the air this evening, on this day, her ninety-third birthday. Something somewhat private. Something that is hers alone.

Turning full circle in the room, taking in the mementos and remembrances of her life, Katherine Anne Morrow slowly, slowly, so gently lowers herself to the floor on the carpet in the middle of the room. Lying back she gazes up at the ceiling, trailing her sight along the curved front of the room, landing, finally, on the scrolled base of the chandelier. Click, click, click. She taps the toes of her camel colored, buckle shoes. Click, click.

There, now everything is as it should be.
As it always was.
Once upon a time.

BOOK FOUR

GATSBY IV

I deplore the conventional. To do or be because it is conventional should be one of the seven deadly sins. It is one of the surest ways to suffocate the soul.

Tradition, on the other hand, can be quite the opposite. They are not the same thing, you know. And because of that, traditions can actually enrich your soul. Nourish parts of it that may be lacking, thirsting, craving. Tradition conjures rich, full tapestries of life and families and cultures. Heritage and belonging and eternal bonds to that which is greater than ourselves.

Conventional is the tie that binds. An emotional and spiritual corset forever tightening its grip with each blind use.

Ah...I do go on, do I not?

Well...

I have a confession. And confession is good for the soul, yes? Well, if not good, perhaps necessary. In truth, all is not well. Or, perhaps all is well, but I am not. Entirely. You see, my shadow friend, I seem to suffer from a perpetual identity crisis. The question of "Who am I" forever lies at the center of my awareness. For you see, it seems that I am continuously changing; in a terminal state of flux. Like a chameleon trapped in a funhouse, with each step I alter yet again, often before I have an opportunity to completely acknowledge or grow familiar with the previous change. It can be quite maddening. And yet, if I am to be completely truthful, I would be afraid, I think, to cease my constant alterations, to reach a change that is the end and so to change no more. How I am is all I know, and so, as maddening and often times fearful as it may be, it is me. I suppose, in some respect, I am the ultimate child of my surroundings, also forever shifting and moving, transforming into something different, more, worse, better. And as I mentioned before, in a world of progress, speed is of the essence, and so my changes occur rapidly. I am child, goddess, vixen, monk; shy, powerful, exhibitionist, hermit. I am soulful, selfish, wise, empty. I am everything. And I am nothing. I care and I don't. No. That was a lie. Through everything, I care. I care. Please believe that.

Something happened the other day. Something frightfully unsettling for the reason that I seemed to be the only one who experienced it.

I stepped outside in the afternoon into a warm spring wind, sidewalk dappled in sunlight, the first robin of the season hopping beneath the tree outside my building.

("When the red, red robin comes bob-bob-bobbing along...")

Before I could take one step I became aware that I had no sense of the sky. No sense that there was anything beyond the towering cement columns all around me. Suddenly, in my mind, my heart, down into the origins of my soul, there was nothing beyond them. And what is more, that ceiling above us all had begun to close in. The sidewalk beneath my feet narrowed as the building in which I live heaved a heavy sigh and inched its way toward the street. Cars parked along the curb came dangerously close to having two tires on the sidewalk itself. And the tops of those monolith towers threw sparks as they scraped the lowering sky.

I needed to draw a full breath but couldn't find the room. I needed to take a great stride forward but felt a baby step was all I was afforded. We were all trapped, suddenly, in a great, monstrous trash compactor, and someone had pushed the button. Like discarded soda cans and milk cartons, we were about to be reduced to flat, manageable packets of unnecessary humanity. Tied into flat, two-dimensional bundles easy to lift and toss aside into the refuse pit.

I knew in my heart that all around me lay magic in the world. Sparks of wonder and fantasy and miracles. But at that moment, the magic seemed little more than an illusion, dealt out by a master before the believing eyes of the child that is me.

I knew that all around me was more. But I couldn't see it.

I couldn't see.

Hah! Darkness comes as easy as dawn, doesn't it? As well as the other way around, which is an important fact to remember.

Fuzzy wuzzy was a bear. Fuzzy wuzzy had no hair. If fuzzy wuzzy had no hair, he wasn't fuzzy, was he?

It is good to laugh. And to cry. I do both often. Occasionally at the same time. That, my dear friend, is my favorite.

Did you know that squirrels use their tails as umbrellas? What an ingenious thing nature is. Why is it, do you suppose that when the rest of the animal kingdom was given various aspects necessary to adapt to life in their environment, humanity was not? Doesn't it seem we have been removed from that process? I mean, do lions and grizzly bears have to go to the dentist? Or floss after every meal? Do gazelles need sunscreen? Oh, I am quite certain one more knowledgeable than I could provide all kinds of rebuttals while delving into a complicated dialogue on just those questions. But I mean them in a much simpler, although no less crucial way. Which came first, the tail or the umbrella? Did we once have one, like the squirrel, until someone discovered that they could string fern leaves together into a kind of awning and hold them up with a stick?

You don't need to answer. In fact, as always, I prefer you do not. I just wonder sometimes how we got the way we are. Perhaps it is just me, but I often feel we have lost something along the way. Such as our humanity.

Ssh. Silence holds all our secrets.

Do you have a favorite color? I don't.

Do you like peanut butter? I do.

Now you know just a little bit more about me. It may seem like it is not nearly enough, but if you have been attentive at all, you will find that it is not entirely true.

And what is more, how much, exactly, is enough?

I know, I make you think a great deal more than you would like to. I'd like to say I am sorry for that, but I am not.

There is very little I am sorry for. Nothing, in fact. Because I think I make you smile a great deal more than you might like as well.

I am Daisy.

Although not really.

I am a great deal more, and so very much less.

Fairly on sweet time doth go,
O'er shining smiles and tears that flow.
T'were nothing more than make believe
Those wishes for time's sweet reprieve.

I wonder sometimes how you feel about me. You out there, silent, shadowed, barely more than a figment of my imagination. I wonder.

Do you mind that I think of you as a friend?

Do you love me? Is that possible? Well, anything is possible, I have learned that much. Have you?

I love...

I love.

That is more, I think, that most can say.

Someday I will find what I am looking for. It may not be until after I have died and left this side of the looking glass, but I will find it.

Oh! I can smell flowers! Sweet, honeyed perfume drifting through my open window. I do not know where the scent is coming from, but in all honesty that is of little concern. None, in fact. Just that pure, unexpected fragrance like a string of pearls dropping one by one from the sky.

It is gone. How wonderful. A brief flicker of coexistence and then a return to solitude. I wish we could have shared that. It would have been nice.

Shoulda, Coulda, Woulda -- the three Sisters of Death.

I'll tell you something else. Because that is what I do. Had you figured that out yet?

I believe that the line between darkness and light, that edge where the fall of the streetlight reaches its end, or between the setting sun and the night shadows, or any other place you find light on one side and shadow on the other, to be the doorway to heaven.

If you find the way to enter that line that is neither dark nor light or perhaps a perfect combination of the two, you will find yourself released from the chains of this world by passing through the gateway to another. I dare you to stare at that line sometime, see if you do not begin to see something there. A meaning. A life. An escape into sheer serenity. The trick, however, is not to stare with your eyes, but with the very fabric of your being. Ah, perhaps I am now delving too far into the metaphysical. I can hear the darkness out there growing intensely silent. Or are you listening? No matter. I am as adept at conversing on the weather as I am at delving into the caverns of the soul.

It is only that the weather doesn't interest me.

Do you know where I am now?

I am in a rowboat on a serene pond surrounded by lily pads. I recline back on silk and linen pillows and allow one hand to drape into the cool water as I blow cigar smoke up to mix with the puffs of clouds. Great, mothering willows, those immense cocoons of a tree, drip their waterfall branches toward the ground and whisper my name as the breeze caresses their manes.

Behind me on the shore is a small gathering of people, snatches of their conversation carried out across the water and over my head like ripples across the surface.

I am drifting.

Drifting.

I feel something.

A breeze, or breath. But the leaves out my window are still. As still as though they were encased in glass.

But I can feel it. When I close my eyes it is as if it is all around me.

All around me.

And carried within, woven on gentle strands of air, is the crystalline sound of laughter. Or perhaps crying. Wrapped in silk and lilac. Distant and soft. Rose petals and soap bubbles.

It is...

Perhaps...

Softly it washes over me, through me, that nonexistent breeze filled with the echoing sounds of her...

Gleeful and melancholy. Child and woman. Innocence and desire.

Don't go. Not now. It is too magical and wondrous to have all to myself. Some things are too private not to share.

At times, I am one of them.

THE UPSTAIRS WINDOW

Mrs. Hanson was the first to use it when she realized that the moon, when full, hung centered in the top right pane, and the summer evening breezes seemed always to find their way through it.

Nights she would sit, rocking baby Chance to sleep, the bicycle bells, and laughter, and ice cream trucks, the only things that seemed to lull him into sleep. Not singing, not the music box, only the scattered, mingling of sounds from the city street below. So she kept the rocker near the window, and on full moon summer nights, she would sit with her baby boy, both of them soothed and calmed by what lay beyond. And she sang anyway, to herself, as much as the boy.

"Hush little baby, don't say word..."

That's when the townhouse was just that -- a townhouse. Before it was sold, split up, and renovated into apartments.

The upstairs room was Chance's, and as he grew up, he discovered that a water balloon, carefully aimed (or even not so carefully) would collide with anyone standing on the front stoop if dropped from his window.

And he spent many an afternoon with nothing to do but look out that window when one of those water balloons collided with the wrong person.

He spent a lot of time at that window.

But eventually Chance grew up and out, leaving behind his water balloons and little boy antics, off to find his own life and way.

His mother lived there alone for another ten years, leaving Chance his room for whenever he came home to visit, and then suddenly, and without warning, she quietly slipped away one night. In the rocker. Rocking. Beneath a quiet summer moon.

Skye Kenwood rented the apartment on the top floor as soon as the building became available. She didn't mind the four-floor walk-up, she'd rather be above looking down.

It was the windows that drew her to the apartment, mounted in the curved, bay wall of the building, and rising to nearly the ceiling. She knew right away that she would make a bay window seat for the one on the left, where the breeze seemed always to billow the curtains there.

In the spring she would sit on that seat with her sketch pad, looking down on the life below, scurrying and hurrying, like blood vessels through a vein.

Sometimes she would lift the screen and sprinkle bird seed on the small ledge outside, then sit and wait for any takers. Mostly there were pigeons, but occasionally she fed a sparrow or two, or on a truly fortuitous day, a mourning dove would settle there and coo his melancholy song.

But moments as such would last only as long as her ambitious feline remained ignorant of the potential prey's existence.

Skye soon found there were fewer places she'd rather be than on her perch, nestled on pillows, watching the world in its never-ending, maddening ballet.

Skye made her home there for nearly four years, painting the molding around the windows, hanging stained glass ovals where the morning sun would have little choice but to pass through them on its way to her sofa.

She painted what she saw outside the window, and what she thought she saw, or wished, or dreamed, and those paintings caught somebody's eye, and before she knew it came the time to move on. But it had served her well, that home. It had cared for her, comforted her, inspired her.

And she left the window seat as a gift to the next person passing through.

To say Neil had been through a tough time would be like saying that when a cow was slaughtered she'd had a bad day.

He had gotten off with the minimum, the whole affair being his first offense and the fact that the judge decided he was basically a good kid who got caught up in a bad situation.

Everyone said they were very impressed with the fact that Neil hadn't let the whole thing drag him down too much. They were glad to hear that he was eager to get his life back on track.

Unfortunately, moving back home was out of the question. He didn't seem to have much of a family anymore. Not now.

So he rented the top apartment because it was the least

expensive one. With his asthma, he wasn't too keen on the four flight walk-up, but we don't always get what we want. He knew that better than anyone.

He swiped a couple of milk crates from a grocery store because he didn't own anything. All he had was his duffel bag of clothes, some CDs, a player, and a T.V. a friend of his gave him.

The first night there he sat in the window nearly the whole night, not knowing quite what to do next, part of him wishing he was still locked up. At least there he didn't have to worry about making any decisions. At least there he wasn't alone, even if he wanted to be. He laughed. When he was there, he'd have given his right arm for a couple of hours totally alone. Now he wished he could hear just one other voice.

But then again, it was the silence that gave him all the time he needed to think. All the time he needed to sit on the little window seat in front of the immense window and put together his plans. Ideas of where and how his life could go if he put his mind to it.

It was the perfect place to sit and read, and for hours on end he would do just that, discovering books like they had just magically appeared in the world for the very first time.

And sure enough, all that reading got him back into school, and a few years later he graduated with honors. And with a brand new job that paid him enough to move into a place where he didn't need to wheeze himself half to death climbing the stairs.

Slowly the building began to empty out. Families moved, rents skyrocketed, maintenance costs went through the roof.

Old tenants tried in vain to have is saved as an historical

landmark, but other than their own, private, personal histories -- Mrs. Hanson and Chance, Skye and then Neil, there was nothing, the city claimed, worth saving.

People's memories aren't worth much in today's market.

So the demolition team moved in and set up their monster machines, getting ready to make way for something newer and better.

A small crowd gathered a short distance away to watch the spectacle including three separate, yet distinct faces, all unaware of one another. Unaware that they shared the same, mournful expression.

And to this day, if you were to pass any of them on the street and ask them, they would swear that the wrecking ball that day had to hit that window three times before it would let go. And even then it dislodged slowly, as though ripping out its roots, and then fell in a slow, graceful arc to the ground, the glass shattering in a spray of prisms reflecting in the sun.

TOO MUCH TOO HOLD

Jeannette McFarland eases her two hundred and fifty pounds onto the sofa hearing the springs flatten beneath her and channel hops between the home shopping network and a 'Brady Bunch' rerun. God bless remotes. What the hell did she do before they were invented? Well, she was skinny then, first of all, so getting up and down to change the channel wouldn't have been such a chore.

She thinks about the weekly conversation with her mother she had earlier, how she says the same thing every time, "Jeanette, you are such a pretty woman, if you'd just drop the weight I'm sure you'd find someone nice." And she says the same thing every time in return, "Mom, they're all just afraid because I'm too much to hold."

The 'Brady Bunch' rerun is one she's seen a thousand times so she contemplates the gold snake bracelet going fast on the shopping network but that would mean getting up to get her credit card and she can't recall exactly where it is anyway.

Besides, by the time she finds it and gets back to the phone they'll be sold out. There -- they're sold out now. Good thing she didn't waste her time.

From where she sits the mantelpiece across the room is visible over the top of the television and her gaze wanders there now, catching on the framed picture of a devilishly handsome man in jeans and green barn coat leaning on the hood of a jeep the same pine color. He is smiling, the sun making him squint little lines around his eyes and his wavy brown hair is blown ridiculously up on one side in the summer breeze. It doesn't seem like a whole year has gone by. She can remember as clearly as if it was yesterday kissing him Happy New Year, drunkenly toasting their glasses so hard that they both shatter sending champagne spilling down their arms and laughter through their hearts. She can remember as clearly as if it was yesterday except for the fact that it was one year and one hundred and twenty-five pounds ago.

The smile in the photo begins to burn so bright it scorches her eyes, making them tear and hurt. Looking away, she retrieves a cookie from the bag on the end table not even tasting it before swallowing and returning to the channel-hopping business at hand.

The noon news is about to begin which makes her think she should have some lunch, but the kitchen is so far away right now, and the sun has reached its slant directly across the couch where she sits, all warm and fuzzy. That would be comforting except for the fact that it also strikes the picture on the mantle, lighting it as if it were coming to life, and again she is drawn to the figure there. She should move it, take it down, put it somewhere else.

Suddenly she is embarrassed, wondering what he would think if he saw her now. His beautiful, loving, adventurous wife, only a year after the jeep she had never wanted because it seemed so like a toy was flattened at an intersection, his green barn jacket and jeans and electric smile smashed between the two sides as they came together like a garbage compactor. He never felt a thing, they said.

But she did.

So no one ever really said anything when things seemed to take a turn for her. When she stopped going out as much or laughing as hard, or when the tears came so easily and often, and the food just always seemed to be around. No one ever said anything when she looked a little tired, or a little heavier, and the circles under her eyes seemed a little more permanent. It was horrible, they said. They'd had their whole lives to look forward to, they said.

They wouldn't understand, anyway. And when someone did begin to speak up, when her mother began expressing her intense motherly concern, Jeannette tried to explain that it was simply that when he died, all the love she had for him, all the love she had planned to give him until the end of time, simply began building up inside her, a balloon filling with air, and she had such an overabundance of it, with nowhere for it to go, that it had no choice but to swell inside her. There was no escape hatch for it, and it had been too much for her skinny little body to hold.

She was fully aware that it could fill her so much that she'd explode from it, blow up with a deafening shot like the Hindenburg, but what could she do? It was all for him and now he was gone and it had nowhere to go.

Besides, there are worse things that could happen. Worse than exploding from too much love. You could be flattened between the doors of a forest green jeep.

She looked at the sun-drenched photo and smiled, feeling herself puff up just a little more.

And on the home shopping network, a porcelain ballerina had just gone on sale, and 'Friends' was on cable.

ROADKILL

Sid nearly drove right by it, both the road and his brain being so fogged in. Damn valleys hung onto it like it was gold. So he almost missed it entirely. Almost. But the peripheral vision of his subconscious caught sight of the neon A-One Motel sign just in time, and he squealed into the parking lot, stopping at the front office. Left the motor running.

Thirty seconds later he backed the car up and dragged his road weary Chevy dangerously fast over the speed bumps in the drive around to the back of the building. Number sixteen. Even numbers on top. There, near the corner. Light on, curtains drawn. He parked the car. Didn't leave it running this time. Nearly locked his keys in it.

Now. Standing beneath the room, sounds of passing traffic coming from the other side of the building. From the highway. Only two other cars parked. One of them hers. Chill creeping down from the hills. Now.

For the entire trip from the city, he'd gone over it again and again. For the entire trip, he'd rehearsed everything. For however many miles he'd been driving, staring at the white lines on the road like a strobe light. Damn! Should have written it down. Adrenaline was the great Mind Paralyzer. Couldn't remember a single bit of it now. Now.

But he could remember lots of other things. Things from longer ago than the hours he'd spent driving. He remembered things he didn't want to remember because it made it hard for him to breath.

Now!

To his right were the stairs leading up to the second level. To his right. Okay. God, he was tired all of a sudden. Just wanted to curl up in the front seat and grab some shut eye. But, that always happened when he got nervous. Get keyed up, want to sleep. Strangest damn thing. Had no idea where that started.

Didn't much care.

On the landing midway up the stairs, he had to stop and catch his breath. Wasn't that tough a climb. What, maybe fourteen steps in all? But his damn heart wouldn't slow down. Beating way too fast for him to catch up. Probably have a heart attack right there. In the cold and fog, he'd collapse right on the cement stairs. Crumpled in a heap right up until morning. That would be a fine wake-up call for the maid.

At the door. Hospital green. Made him think he smelled ammonia. Made him nauseous. Okay. Now. Only thing to do was do it.

He banged on the door three solid times. Louder than he had intended. Adrenalin kicked in.

"Alice? Alice, open the door."

Lights went out. Not very subtle. Did she think he would suddenly think there was no one in there? Or that is wasn't her? For an incredibly intelligent girl, sometimes she wasn't very smart.

And thirty-three years old was far too young for him to be having a heart attack. That reminded him. Tomorrow Alice will turn thirty. He should have brought her something. He looked around where he stood as though a gift or thoughtful gesture would magically appear on the second level of a highway motel. On the ground lay a cigarette butt, a band-aid, and a crumbled piece of paper. Not exactly what he had in mind.

"Alice, c'mon. Will you just open the door?"

An eighteen wheeler barreled down the highway blaring its horn into the night. The ground rumbled. An earthquake might be a nice change of pace. Too bad they were in the wrong part of the country. No tornadoes, no floods, no hurricanes. Nothing worth anything. They were safe.

"Go away." Her husky voice emerged from the darkness.

"Sorry. No can do." He struggled against a yawn. That wouldn't make a very good impression.

A long silence inside and out. He knew there was something he had wanted to begin with. Something to get the ball rolling in the right direction. Something he had wanted her to know.

"Alice, please open the door."

That wasn't it.

The light clicked on again and Sid held his breath. Nothing happened. Sid swatted away a mosquito and noticed he had begun to sweat. Noticed it was hot. How could that be? He wanted a glass of water. Wanted to sleep.

Suddenly the door swung open seemingly by itself, because the minute she flung it, she walked away, leaving it to bounce open alone. Sid caught it on the rebound and stepped in.

Alice sat on the bed with her back to him. He closed the door behind him before the moths swirling around the outside light homed in on the inside one.

She made no move when the door slammed shut.

"I'm thirsty as hell. I need a drink of water." Sid went past her into the bathroom. He ran the water until it was as cold as possible. About room temperature. Unwrapped a plastic cup, filled it, drank it, filled it again and went back to the room. The water left a stale taste in his mouth. Or maybe that was there before.

Alice had moved to the other side of the bed so that her back was still to him. Smoke from a cigarette rose over her head as though her face was on fire.

"How did you know I was here?"

"Just figured it out."

"How?"

"Just did."

Staring at her back, at her hair hanging long and wavy, Sid had the sudden sensation that if she were to turn around now, he'd see some figure from a horror movie. Distorted, grotesque, melting and old.

He drained the water in the glass and tossed the cup in the trash basket. It landed with a *thunk*.

"So, Alice, what is it exactly that you're doing here?"

"Nothing." She waved away a bug that Sid couldn't see.

"I see, nothing?"

"Yes. Nothing."

"And why is it that you had to come all the way here to do it? Or, not do it, as the case may be."

"Sid, what do you want?" She reached toward the end table and stubbed out her cigarette in the ashtray there. To do so, Sid got just a glimpse of her left ear and part of her jawbone.

"I want you to come home." He tried to think if that would be his first question if he was her. He tried but failed.

"I can't do that right now."

"Why not?"

"You wouldn't understand."

"How do you know that if you won't tell me!" He hadn't meant to raise his voice, but he was awfully tired of looking at the back of her head.

"Don't yell at me."

"Fine, " he lowered his voice to a controlled conversational tone, "how do you know if you won't tell me."

"Sid, just go home."

"Sorry. No can do." In all honesty, Sid felt a nearly uncontrollable urge to smack her so hard that her head spun around like a top. He also wanted to bury his face in her hair until it suffocated him. He did neither. He did the only thing he didn't want to do which was to stand completely still.

Alice raised her hands to her face, either pulling her eyeballs out or trying to massage the tension from them. "Ow -- dammnit!" And she was off the bed and on the floor as though pulled from below.

"What's wrong?" Sid started toward her, thinking for a moment that perhaps she did dislodge an eyeball from its socket, and it now rolled around beneath the bed.

"I dropped my contact lens."

"Well, here, I'll help you." He moved around to the other side of the bed.

"Wait -- " She moved to interfere with his step, but failed. "Pick up your foot for chrissake!"

"What!" he did as she ordered.

She reached forward to where he had stood a second before and retrieved an almost invisible object. "You stepped on it."

"Oh...I'm sorry, Alice. I'm -- "

"You see! You see what happens when you can't just leave well enough alone?" She was up now. Facing him. No horror movie face. Just those shocking blue eyes piercing through him.

"What? What?" he pleaded. God, he loved her so much, couldn't she see that?

"Just leave me alone!" She collapsed to the bed again, contact lens enclosed in her hand.

"Alice..." He tried to embrace her.

"Do you know that all the way here I kept seeing one dead animal after another on the side of the road? A raccoon, a possum, something unidentifiable flattened against the asphalt run over God knows how many times by cars, trucks, and rigs. And the more I saw, the harder it hit me. That's how I feel."

"I -- " Sid faltered.

"Like roadkill. Like something run over again and again and again with no time to mend in between until I'm nothing but a smear of guts and blood and mess slowly being burned into the asphalt."

She got up and went to the bathroom to clean her lens. Sid sat on the bed. Alone. Now.

Now, now, now.

"Alice?"

"What."

"I love you."

The water stopped running and Alice emerged wiping her hands on her jeans. "I know that, Sid. But it's not enough."

He could've gotten a room, he supposed, but somehow he preferred to sleep in the car. He reclined the seat and stared at the window of her room until he fell asleep.

He dreamed of animals. Raccoons with their ringtails and masked eyes. Their backs to him. Turning around to reveal the horror movie face of Alice.

When he woke the next morning, her car was gone and the door to her room was open. Maid's cart beside it.

Happy Birthday, Alice.

He keyed the ignition and drove slowly over the speed bumps, paused for a car and trailer on the highway, then pulled back out in the direction he had come.

The fog hung low in the early morning air, as though the clouds had suddenly grown tired and needed to rest in the cool grass and morning dew.

About twenty miles down the highway, he hit the brakes, tried to swerve, but was afraid he hadn't seen the poor thing hobbling toward the side of the road in time. Damn fog. He closed his eyes when he heard the thump, his stomach going sour almost immediately.

He pulled to the side of the road and looked behind him, tail lights shining eerily into the mist. Yup. He had hit it alright. It was dead now, stomach poking out onto the road. Tongue out. Blood. It was dead now.

He turned around again and leaned his head on the steering wheel, not quite expecting the tears that came. His head hurt. And his stomach. And other, less physical things too.

Putting the car back into gear, he pulled slowly back out onto the road. He'd just have to be more careful. Drive slow all the way back if he had to.

As least until the fog lifted.

That's all. Just go slow and careful. Whatever it took to keep that from happening ever again.

Once was more than enough.

FOR EXAMPLE

Take this exact moment, for example.

She is laying on the floor, the hardwood conflicting with her tailbone, her head propped on a throw pillow she was sure she'd never use but couldn't bring herself to ever throw away.

The sky is bluer and more perfect than she can remember anything being in her entire life, and the sun so present she thinks for a brief, but passing, moment that she should be outside, squarely in its wash. But the floor is hard, the pillow soft, and the contradiction is comforting to her. As is the cigarette that burns threateningly close to the filter, the smoke curling and twisting like the mist just before the Genie appears from the lamp. She wishes he would.

She drinks long from her lemonade, upset that she has to sit up to do so because she likes the way the world looks from her position on the floor. But what she likes more is the way the vodka in the lemonade dulls the hardness of the floor, softens the brightness of the sun, twists the passing of time, and makes the thoughts of him warm and soft and wonderful, even if they do bring tears.

She wonders, from her position on the floor, why more time isn't spent in this position. The world is nice from here. Comforting, distant, far above and easy to turn away from.

But that isn't really what she wants.

She stares at the phone with a will stronger than God's, all the while praying for the harsh, grunge music pouring from her stereo to increase the numbness in her heart.

Life is just the time you pass in between complications.

Life is just the time passed in between funerals. She heard that on some TV show. Why does she think of that now?

She shifts her position on the floor, liking the discomfort on her hipbone and her spine. Well, not liking it exactly, but acknowledging it. It is real. Present. Current. Not some distant, unattainable mirage. She stubs out her cigarette and lights another one. She doesn't know what else to do.

What, for example, is he doing at this exact moment? Is he consumed with the insane, incessant, seemingly unfounded, confounding, resounding, inescapable, irreplaceable feelings she is plagued with? Blessed with? Haunted by? Ee-ii-ee-ii-o.

Take for example the way that it seemed to her that the whole world had stopped except for the fact that she can see the slant of the sun change positions, the clock tick laborious moment after moment, her breath rise and fall ad infinitum, while her position on the hardwood floor does not shift except for an occasional drag on cigarette, or drink of lemonade.

The music on the stereo begins to make her nervous. The wood floor makes her think unthinkable things. For example;

late nights, too many candles, too much to drink, too much said, too little done, and long, lonely nights of wishing.

It must be near dinner time. She should eat. But she does not want to move from her place. She likes it there. So much that she wishes, for a moment, that she could live her whole life from a place where she could see the easy perfection of a cool blue sky, the distinction of shadow and sun, and the reality of hardwood beneath her. Simple, clear, and definite. But life's lessons have proven tenfold that that is far, far, too much to ask. We learn from our trials, isn't that so? Without them, with nothing but clear simplicity, we would be forever ignorant. But -- what is it they say about ignorance?

But it is always more complicated than that. Take, for example, all the muscle coordination, and sheer force of will it takes to get out of bed every morning. It is much easier to stay right where you were the night before, yet something propels us to exert the force necessary anyway. What? Survival? Responsibility? Desire? Suddenly none of them seem enough to drive her up from the floor. She prefers its sweet, basic existence.

Except for the lack of him. That is the complication. Perhaps that will be enough to send her to her feet. Or, perhaps, the sensation will pass and she will spend the remainder of her days in blissful compliance with tobacco and vodka.

The phone rings. Not shrill and loud as one might expect in the near perfect silence of the afternoon, but soft and cooing. Just a gentle reverberation of sound. She recalls, vaguely, having focused so much of her energy and attention on it earlier that she thought she had lost her very soul to it. And now it sings to her. Two, three times. The sound spins through the cigarette smoke and spiked lemonade. She hears it in her bones. Her heart. It is a soothing, comforting sound and yet she wonders now if it is enough to force her to leave a place she has grown so fond of.

SNOW

Cyrano, as we called him because of his nearly tangible shyness and unfailing romanticism, began an amorous relationship with his beer bottle, lovingly undressing it, peeling off the label as attentively and carefully as one would remove the nightgown of a virgin bride. Ian and I watched for only a moment, then toasted our slices of lime before sending our shots of tequila into the depths of our souls. It dulled the spike of life, reminded us that we needn't be concerned with anything more complicated than now. Nothing before, certainly nothing later.

Cyrano, (his real, or birth, name, was Jerry and fit him about as well as a hand-me-down suit from a shorter, fatter sibling) took the delicately removed label and slapped it to his forehead. He was not a drinker. Ian and I were. Separately and together. We believed in shared separateness, and little else.

Ian was the love of my life in as much as a stiff drink and harsh music was the love of my spirit. Destructive? Maybe.

Inspiring? Absolutely. Numbing? Thank God! And he was Cyrano's ex. It is the 90's. We had gathered in my apartment to bid farewell to Cyr, as he was hopping a plane in the morning for parts unknown. No plan. No thought. Just pure idea and intense desire.

"So, Cyr?" I took a swig of Ian's beer as a chaser. He looked incredulous and rose to get me my own from the fridge.

"Yes, Laura?"

"Alaska."

"Absolutely."

Ian returned with my very own bottle of beer. "Here you go, lover." He kissed me hard. He kissed me long. And even through the beer and tequila, I could feel Cyrano's stare. Normally he would look away. Beer made him bold. That, and perhaps, knowledge of his imminent departure.

"You two are the best couple I've seen in a long time."

"You think so?" I didn't know whether to be insulted or flattered. Had it come from my mother, I'd have been insulted -- downright horrified. But from Cyr, I suppose it was okay.

I dragged off my beer and poured three shots of tequila. I missed one glass and poured it on the floor.

"Yup. Better than Ian and *I* were."

"Why do you say that?" Ian handed him a shot.

"I don't know. There's a light about you now. I think, Ian, for the first time you are truly in love."

That word. There was that word. What did it mean again? I wanted to reach for the dictionary. Now it would keep me up all night.

"I think -- " Ian sloshed an arm over my shoulder, "I think you are right."

"Yeah, well, you're also drunk." I removed his arm before he spilled my drink. I had my priorities straight. But I did run my tongue along the line of his ear.

"Yeah. Me too. I need to sit down." Cyr swallowed more beer.

"You *are* sitting down," I said.

And we laughed, us three, strange and close friends. Friends that had been for so very long we were more family. And I thought again of Cyrano flying off to Alaska, that last frontier, for reasons he hadn't shared even with us. Or, perhaps, there was no reason. That was reason enough.

I wished I had the nerve, the bravado, the romanticism to drop it all and strike out with nothing but impulse and faith. I did have the knowledge of nothing to lose, and the feline ability to always land feet first. Perhaps I was on the right track.

"I'd like to propose a toast!" Ian lifted his shot glass. "To the wild wanderer. Too shy to look you in the eye, but he'll move to the tundra with nothing but a ski hat and a dream."

"Well, the ski hat at least." Cyr rose his glass high.

We clinked glasses and shot them back. The room wavered as I set my glass on the floor and I grabbed Ian's sleeve. "Yeah, Cyr, what is this dream of yours?"

He looked at me then, his eyes changing color, and he looked clear through me. I could feel his gaze penetrate every cell and fiber of me, and in fact felt I was disintegrating under his spell. I clenched my fists and laughed to re-establish my solidity.

"Hey -- " Cyrano rose and went past me to the window, "It's starting to snow."

Ian didn't seem to notice the total and unmistakable shift in Cyrano. He simply poured a shot and finished his beer, going to the fridge for another. I forgot him and turned to the window.

"Cyr?"

"Have you ever stood outside in the middle of a snowstorm, Laura?"

"No. I don't think I have." But I had. Why did I say I hadn't?

"This city, believe it or not, becomes almost silent. Silent. Without sound. It's like the snow is natural soundproofing, cushioning everything. And the whole world falls silent. Ssh. Like being wrapped in a ton of blankets. Like slowly, blissfully, going deaf. Like dying."

Ian stopped in the middle of the room, beer in hand, and trained his gaze on his ex-boyfriend. I remained on the floor, booze forgotten, captivated by the world Cyrano saw. Wondered where it existed. Where I saw bleak, Cyr saw magic.

"Like *what*?" Ian ran his free hand through his hair. He was nervous.

"Like dying. Like death. Like -- "

"Like what, Cyr?" I ran my hand along Ian's calf. He was there.

"I have AIDS. I'm dying."

I remember, somehow, not being surprised.

We counted to three and shot another round back together, laughing at something I can't remember now, the lights off, watching the snow fall heavier, thicker, big lazy, snowflakes tumbling past the window and adding to the piles already gathered on the sidewalks, the cars, the fire escape. I thought maybe the whole world would be buried, frozen, and we'd all fall silently to sleep leaving the world to start over. I hoped.

Ian had retreated somewhere inside, and except for the occasional glance around the room and stroke of my cheek, I think he was lost in fear. Or just lost. I fought tears, hot and cruel. Tears for Cyr, for us, for a world so lost and dark and beautiful outside my window. Cyrano kept shouting, "Here's to the unknown! To adventure! To dying and Alaska and snowfalls that last forever! I can't wait for any of them." That's what it all was for him -- an adventure.

We turned on the radio and Cyr asked Ian to dance with him, and as I watched I saw how much Cyrano still loved Ian. And I thought, if that's true, he must still love life, too. But he didn't look sad. He didn't look angry. He looked -- he looked like all of us. Like any of us. Just another guy who'll go to sleep tonight a little drunk, a little scared, a little content, wake up tomorrow with a mix of daring and dread, get through the day whatever way he could, and repeat it all again and again until the day he died. For him, that was just a little sooner.

(a different)
ONCE UPON A TIME...

I have a memory. One to go with all the others crowded and suffocating inside.

I am twenty-two. I have been out of school for several years having gotten restless and anxious to be on my way and so dropped out with one year to go. No lectures. Thank you.

I have a memory, a story of long ago and far away. A Once Upon A Time...

I live in a world of leather jackets and late nights. Underground bars and torn stockings. I am an actress in New York living with a musician. It is the ultimate cliché. It is the tragedy of struggle for your blood love, your only desire, your do or die. Together we are our statement. Our short story. On the streets we get stares, people swearing we are someone they should know. "Isn't he...isn't she...?" We laugh. Our leather jackets rubbing closely together, my cowboy boots jutting sharply from beneath my torn jeans. We are the ultimate artistic couple. Loving what we are pursuing, willing to risk it all, sacrifice it all. Loving each other, willing to be it all, risk it all. How romantic.

I am twenty-two, living in a dark, passionate world known only to musicians, vampires, and the lost ones who find their solace in packs of Marlboro and bottles of bud. (Which one am I?)

Even now, sitting alone at the bar, praying another of our friends will show up to join me, even now, I am present, but not part of this crazy, two a.m. crowd. (I am none of them) Even now I sit, ashtray guarded before me, Budweiser snuggled in my fist, and except for the one I came with, I do not understand any of what I sit among. I look out across the dank, tight length of the bar and wonder why they are all here. I wonder what they talk about. I wonder how it feels to them when the last cigarette is stubbed out and the last beer drained, and they have to go home. I look out across the dank, tight length of the bar and suddenly they are all so very far away. I panic, my first brush with this feeling; I have been set adrift from the mothership, nothing to tether me to safety. I watch helplessly as they slip farther away, my only salvation being to cling to the bar's edge, hoping it is elastic enough to stretch as they recede, fearing at any moment it might snap, sending me spinning off into nothingness.

I am wondering what made me feel all that as the bar snaps back into place at the touch of my loving musician's hand. I wonder what made all that so suddenly, desperately important and heightened and focused as the jukebox blasts, and red lipstick smears piles of Marlboro filters and beer bottle necks. I wonder as the smell of leather mixes with sweat and wet ashtrays, and outside it begins to rain.

"Sometimes I feel so sad. I mean, sad the way it is really meant. Not all weepy and crying, but all the way down in the pit of me, I feel sadness." I look to him, standing with me beneath the slight awning of a Korean deli, and for a second -- only the briefest second in all of eternal time -- I forget why I love him. I look out into the rain from our two-foot haven of dryness and when his arms come around from behind, the sleeves of his leather squeaking against mine, his fingers interlacing mine, his words, "I love you" in my ear, I forget what I had forgotten.

And we are as always. Two to change the world. Two to play by our rules, no compromise, no yielding. We are fireworks inside a shoebox, busting out, exploding, painting flashes of stars in the sky.

We are poets, dreamers, shadows of life, alone together in the strange, mixed-up, misunderstanding world. That is our bond. Our fire.

We are together for a long time, in passion, in anger, in laughter. Together we traverse and explore the razor edge of existence, knowing there is much to fear, thrilled by the possible dangers.

I am moving, constantly moving, shoving as much life inside of me as possible with little care or concern. I am full. I am whole. We are all that there is.

And suddenly, there is *more*. Suddenly, I am not so full. I am more fear than excitement, more lost than exploring.

We sit together in our apartment, he and I, as we always do, and I am struck by the thought that I do not know who he is. No, I correct myself, it is *myself* that I do not know. And like the swift and total crack of a whip, for the first time I am afraid that if I were to look in the mirror, the face there would be a stranger to me.

So I do.

But it is the same. At least, I remember the same reflection being there the previous day. But who was that as well?

I come back and sit beside him, apparently looking pained and pale because he asks, "Are you alright?"

I look at him, hoping something in his eyes, his face, his expression will remind me. Who I am.

There is nothing.

I look around the living room at my things, praying now, hoping against hope, fingers and toes crossed that something there will remind me.

Nothing.

I am not the books on my shelves or the pointe shoes on the wall. I am not the typewriter with the third page of chapter two held within it, I am not the sketches I attempt in my notebook. I am not my leather jacket or my cowboy boots. I am not who he sees me as.

I am panicking. There is no sign of me anywhere. Where have I gone?

"Hey, what's wrong?"

"I am a lie."

I have that memory in me, vivid as if it were yesterday, although I am not sure it is true. Just the same I am not sure it isn't. But it is there. It lives. True or imagined, it remains, crawling and prowling the unlit caverns of my psyche, waiting its turn. Waiting for a blast of a subway train roaring

173

past, or the splash of a taxi careening through a puddle, or another's hand slipped silently into mine -- to remind me.

But for now, at least, it is simply a Once Upon a Time.

AND FINALLY, GATSBY

One day I will wake. As if from a long forgotten slumber, I will open my eyes to find the misty shroud has been removed and all will come clear. One day I will wake, but for now, I float lackadaisically; a lily on a pond, summer's easy breath sending gentle, loving ripples across the surface. Lily. A name nearly as close to a sigh as Daisy. Human flora. Those who move through the world barely stirring the air. So ethereal as to almost move between the molecules around them with nary a disturbance. And yet, their presence is undeniable. Their quiet perfection and simple beauty, breathtaking. They disturb almost nothing and yet are rarely ever forgotten.

Well, I am the hopeless romantic, aren't I?

I suppose I could blame the moon. It is full and large and luminous tonight. I find it difficult to breathe on nights such as this. It seems the intensity of the shining moon steals the oxygen. Drinking it in I become drunk. Not boisterous, liquor drunk, just soft, fuzzy champagne drunk. Giddy.

Oh, my friend, I would that you could see the things I see. I would lend you my eyes, were it possible, but in truth that would do no good. You'd need my soul, and if I were to lend you that, I would die.

Will you remember me once we have parted? I shall remember you. Oh, yes, I will glimpse you in all the things I see for the rest of my days.

There is an old lighthouse across the river, its dead silhouette barely discernible in the darkness. How long ago did its light penetrate the deathly blackness? How many lives did it save?

Don't they need it anymore? Are there no more lives to be watched over? No more souls to save? I wonder.

But there it stands, poor old thing, alone, peaceful, serene. Lonely, perhaps? No, not with so many to look and appreciate it. And yet, it stands neglected, no use for its gifts any longer. Sad. It is an old man, perched at the edge of the water, gazing out at each passing dawn and dusk, waiting for time to finally take its ultimate toll, chiseling away mortar by stone until it crumbles to dust beneath its weight. Time is immensely heavy, you know. Have you never noticed? You will notice now. It is heavy.

But the moon is light. It is a bubble forever floating overhead, reminding us of wonder and mystery. Can you feel it? If not it means you've lost all your innocence and I grieve you that. That is a horrible, monstrous loss that I'm not certain can ever be recovered from. Although I suppose it is always worth a try. Almost anything is.

I have tried, for instance, to imagine what it might be like to be you. However, I know so little about you that I failed almost instantly. And yet, I know enough to feel I might succeed. I love to imagine what it would be like to be other people. But I fear that sometimes I imagine so strongly I lose sight of who I am. Indeed, who I am now may only be a strange combination of all my imaginings. And yet, aren't we all, to some degree, a product of our imaginations? When we were young we said, "I want to be that when I grow up." We pattern ourselves after those we admire. Or opposite of those we don't.

There I go again. Masquerading as philosopher and intellectual. It is entertaining though -- the occasional masquerade. Don't you think? Perhaps not. But I do. And this is my world you are in now. Or, am I in yours? Interesting question. Perhaps in joining together we are creating, and therefore sharing, yet a third world. Oh, everything is such a fantastic puzzle! There is no end to its fascination! No end that I can see.

Death is always over your left shoulder. Did you know that? I love to tell you things you do not already know. It is there, that shadow sometimes glimpsed out of the corner of your eye. But when you turn to it, it is gone. Cherish that, my friend. It is a gentle reminder. If you ask of what, I am afraid it is already too late.

I want to be forever. Timeless and eternal as the printed words on this page. Captured and preserved and everlasting. Too grand a desire, do you suppose? Well, we must have grand desires. It is what propels us onward. And so I desire the grandest of grand. That is always my aim. I told you, fairytales and daydreams and the great American novel.

Dream, dream, dream! Lift your eyes above the senselessness and rain, lift your gaze to the heavens that have always hovered overhead. There is but one cloud in the sky, leaving the sun free to dance off the wing of the seagull that tips its cap to the lighthouse over the river. There is a gentle, singing breeze which carries the laughter of young and old, the cries of the lonely and afraid, and together they mingle into a passionate aria of life.

So, I am a freak. I read constantly and avidly. For no apparent reason I am often, and crucially, wounded by the plight of my fellow man and yet inspired by her spirit. I am saddened and fearful at the state of our world, and disillusioned and disappointed by the general human attitude. I am greatly moved by and angry for our children, awed and humbled by the sense of something greater than us all, nearly always happy, sad, hurt, enraged, all simultaneously, and even in the darkest, most horrific moments, I am in love.

And so, I am.

Forever the outcast. Forever on the proverbial outside looking in. Never with my nose pressed against the glass, mind you. Oh, no. I am not that eager or desperate to pass through to the other side. But I am, like Gatsby, sitting at the edge of the water gazing wistfully, thoughtfully, soulfully out at the green light at the edge of the dock on the other side.

Oh, my friend, you probably think me silly and foolish and strange. I don't mind, really. You may think whatever you like. I will simply blow cigar smoke out into the unfathomable dark.

And I will share with you my greatest secret of all. It is my one, true, inescapable fear. It is the fear of one day finding the truth to be this:

"He had come a long way to this blue lawn, and his dream must have seemed so close he could hardly fail to grasp it. He did not know it was already behind him, somewhere back in that vast obscurity beyond the city..."

F. Scott Fitzgerald: The Great Gatsby

Farewell, my shadow friend. I shall miss you and think of you often; as I gaze at the spinning current of the river, each time I pass an upended trash can, its contents strewn like urban rose petals lightly across my path, in every child blowing streams of opalescent soap bubbles that find their way up to my fire escape...in the glow of the street light, scrap of paper in a puddle, sunset reflecting off the cold steel of the Brooklyn Bridge. I shall think of you.

And I ask only one thing in return -- every once in a while when the night is dark and quiet and blue, light a cigar, blow the smoke out into the silence...

...and think of me.

About the Author

Melissa Volker started out as an actress after attending NYU and the Strasberg Institute for theater. After fourteen years of chasing the dream of stage and screen in NYC, she opted for a more sane and stable life, and moved to Boston.

There, she spent time figuring out what life-not-as-an-actress would look like, and discovered a creative outlet in writing beginning her first novel in earnest while working as an office manager for a firm in Cambridge. During quiet days, lunch hours, and snuck moments between employee training, supply ordering and company meetings, she wrote as fast as the words came. She wrote late into the night, over coffee in the morning, while riding the T, and whenever there was spare time.

Boston is also where met her husband, Christopher, and five years into their marriage they had a son.

Melissa currently lives in Western MA with her family, life-schooling (homeschooling, but not schooling-at-home) their son, and has expanded her creative life into photography, finding that sometimes stories are told in words, other times, in pictures.

You can visit her online at **www.melissavolker.com** to see her photos and her other writing. Subscribe to her free newsletter to receive occasional essays, sneak-peeks, and information on upcoming events and works.

Also by Melissa Volker

"Delilah of Sunhats and Swans"
a literary novel

"The Thirteenth Moon: A Moya Fairwell Adventure"
a youn teen fantasy adventure novel

Anabelle Lost
YA thriller

HIDDEN: an impossible story
YA magical realism

For more information, and to stay up to date:
www.melissavolker.com